DEVIL-IN-
THE-FOG

YEARLING BOOKS/YOUNG YEARLINGS/YEARLING CLASSICS are designed especially to entertain and enlighten young people. Charles F. Reasoner, Professor Emeritus of Children's Literature and Reading, New York University, is consultant to this series.

For a complete listing of all Yearling titles, write to Dell Readers Service, P.O. Box 1045, South Holland, Illinois 60473.

DEVIL-IN-THE-FOG

Leon Garfield

A Yearling Book

To Vivien

· 1 ·

MY FATHER is put in the stocks again! Oh! The injustice of it! My father is a genius—as are all of we Treets. A grand man, as great in mind as he is in body, for he's a large man who bears himself with more dignity than all the Justices in Kent put together. Except when the Stranger calls, and then his spirit seems to flicker and sink somewhat . . . as if the Stranger was something dark and devilish, and there was an unwholesome bargain eating away at my father's soul. . . .

He comes on the third day of June and November—to Rye or Sandwich (it used to be Faversham, but that's changed, now)—and is always unseasonable . . . though fog and damp suits him better than high summer. Not that he's ever been seen in the sun. After dark—always. Between nine and ten o'clock, when the lesser Treets are abed and the inn parlor's empty of all save my father and me. We sit by the fire (if there is one) and wait, and my father's grand spirit begins to flicker. A strained look comes over his powerful face, and all his thoughts seem sunk in his boots. Gone's the bright look of invention in his eyes, and the mind that's produced the most remarkable stage effects our age has known is no more lively than stale beer. Then the Stranger comes, with his cold, uncanny stare at me; the business is done—and he goes off into the night. My father bids me "good night"—even blesses me—and a bad day's done. On the next morning, he's Mr. Thomas Treet again—and the world's a better place for that.

All our lives, this man's been coming—till there were times when we Treets thought it as natural to have a Stranger in the family as a hole in one's stocking—by which I mean, everyone's had one, but no one boasts about it.

Sometimes, on the road, we'd see some grim-faced, watery-eyed gentleman in brown or black, sitting formidably in a fast coach, and say:

"There goes someone else's Stranger! Worse than ours, ain't he!"

Then we'd trundle on and forget him entirely in the eternal excitement of our triumphs to come.

We traveled from town to town and from inn to inn in a grand canvas wagon—a snuff-colored world under a snuff-colored sky. Six within, and two without—depending on the weather: when it rained, and we were between towns, in some sodden old Kentish lane, then there'd be eight within—among the hoists and jars and baskets and crucibles . . . with Otway's head coming in at the back, like a gentleman amazed by geniuses. (Otway was our horse.)

Then, while the rain rattled and thumped down on our sky—fit to burst it—Mr. Treet would talk of the bright future . . . of enormous glory, even on the London stage. Of which he was never for a moment in doubt. For it was so much a part of my father's nature and spirit always to look forward, and never behind. . . .

"Treets," he'd say. "Never look backward! Never brood upon the past, my dears. For the past's but material for to build the rich future. Would you ever have heard Sir Christopher Wren—God rest his memory!—gazing at his fine churches and saying, 'Ah! But you should have seen the bricks! They were beautiful'?"

Yes, indeed, we're a family with a golden future! I remember once while we were halted by Bodiam Castle, between Tenterden and Rye, and the rain was coming down like grapeshot, a drenched highwayman demanded shelter. He thumped on the wagon's side, then stuck his head in at the back like an uprooted bush with two red berries for eyes.

"Vagrants!" he said disgustedly, and climbed, unasked, inside.

At first he was surly and blustering and inclined to offer his pistol—which, if he'd fired it, would have discharged no more than half a pint of rainwater.

"What's them poles an' ropes an' pulleys for?"

"Sir, they are flying machines."

He grunted contemptuously, but, nonetheless, looked curiously at the hoists.

"How do they work?"

"They're constructed after the principles of Archimedes, sir, and with certain improvements of my own. They are, so to speak, a cage for the forces of Nature."

He sniffed and stared around into the mysterious gloom—meeting with more pairs of cool, proud eyes than he'd bargained for.

"What's in them baskets?"

"Books, sir, and the properties of our art."

"What properties?" (Was he thinking of robbing us?)

"Wings and crowns and angels' robes and devils' horns . . . in short, sir—the properties of genius."

Again he sniffed with a show of contempt, but he was somewhat reduced by now—and plainly wondering what manner of world had pocketed him up.

"And what's in them great fat jars—with bellies on 'em like your own?"

Our father is a great man—and greatly built. But not overstout. The highwayman's jibe came more from a need to show himself as terrible than from a just observation.

"In those jars, sir, are all the mysteries and wonders of the natural world. Oil of Sugar! Berlin Syrup! Crystals of Violet! Salts of Fire! Even Crystals of Lemon—dangerous, sir! Fierce and deadly as a tiger! Pilfer but one—even lay your hand on it!—and you'll be frizzled like a burned-out sausage, together with much prosperous smoke besides!"

This was too much for him. He took a last look around at the extraordinary family perched among their dark and solemn paraphernalia—and fled for his miserable life!

Then, when he'd gone—and it was certain he wasn't coming back—our father ventured a tremendous smile. He creaked forward on his basket and gently rubbed his ankles and calves (for he wasn't long out of the stocks at Tenterden).

"Treets," he said. "Consider. If that fierce scoundrel was amazed half out of his wits by only *hearing* of our genius, think, my dears, of the roar and acclaim when we're on the London stage! The magnificence to come, Treets! It dazzles me!"

This was on June the first. On June third—to the Mermaid in Rye—came the Stranger. Nine o'clock in the evening. Bringing a smell of fog and mist and mildewed damp with him. . . . And for that day and the next, my father was in his most somber dumps. . . .

It was then, for the first time, I asked him outright what was the Stranger to us. For his gloom had seemed deeper than ever before—even as his previous dreams had been brighter. He turned to me sadly, laid his hand on my shoulder, and said:

"George, my eldest son . . . George, my firstborn—never ask me that."

He spoke with such solemnity—even tragic dignity—that I was reminded of his performance as the Patriarch Abraham when I played Isaac in the Miracle Play, and Hotspur Treet (the youngest genius of us all) came down from heaven on father's flying machine for to stay the sacrificial hand, while Jane Treet, garbed in curly wool, bleated like a ram from a thicket of father's designing.

The last time we played it was in St. John's Church at Faversham, two years ago when I was twelve and Hotspur was five. And my father was put in the stocks on account of Hotspur's having gone through a window very dear to the church. We've never played in Faversham since . . . which is a sadness to us all, for it was in Faversham our mother died, and is buried there these past seven years. My father—who'd taken a deal of mulled ale at the funeral feast (she died in November; everything disquieting happens in June or November)—remarked sadly to us all that "She flies—ah she flies with better machines than mine, now, my dears!"

From which I received a distinct notion that heaven was filled with a golden profusion of hoists that never broke, nor stuck, nor poked young Treets through stained-glass windows.

Not that flying hoists is my father's chief achievement. Cascades and Fountains; Visions and Apparitions; Dragons and Cherubs; "Lucifer's Smoke" and the "Devil's Fire" . . . there's nothing his spacious mind ain't turned itself to, save flattering the Justices and humbling himself before the landlord. A very proud disposition—like all we Treets—which makes his wretchedness before the Stranger even more sinister . . . and it reaches its darkest when he takes the purse of guineas off him like it was filled with poisonous spiders.

Yet at all other times, even in the stocks, he's as proud as St. Paul's. He sits there, hands on hips, and surveys the idle gapers like he's holding court. One would never suspect the anchored feet with their patched soles belonged to the grand man upon the other side of the locked boards. Vagrant? Disturber of the peace? Mountebank? Who but a mealy-mouthed, jumped-up Justice could call him so? And the insolent landlord of the Eloquent Gentlewoman.

November five—a somber, yellowish day, with a promise of fog—and the Stranger's not been! But the pleasure of his absence has been soured by our father's consequently being unable to pay the landlord for provisions, and being stocked as a "pompous swindler" and an "overbearing vagrant." (Last year it was—"Thank you, Mr. Treet, sir!")

I tell you, if not for that grasping landlord, we Treets would have been dancing for joy! A world without a Stranger? Like a meal without a reckoning! (Never mind the evil guineas!)

"Treets," said Mr. Treet, while he was being locked in, "behold how the common, vulgar world deals with genius! What it cannot understand, it jeers at! Didn't it laugh at Archimedes when his bath overflowed? It did indeed! Fools, idle fools! But we know, my dears"—he stared contemptuously at the landlord—"that one puff of 'Lucifer's Smoke'—"

" 'Lucifer's Smoke'?" sneered that objectionable man—for the stocks was but an egg's throw from the parlor of the inn. "What does a rumpled bumpkin like Mr. Thomas Treet know of it but its name? Eh? Eh? Ha! My bottom's better informed!"

Mr. Treet looked at him with tremendous dignity and said: "Then, sir, you ought to wear your hat on your bottom and put your breeches over your head, for *that's* as ignorant as a pig! Children—tell this unlettered gent what is meant by Treet's 'Lucifer's Smoke' —and the magnificence of it!"

(This last to us, for all seven of us never deserted Mr. Treet when he was in the stocks, but sat upon that hateful object and explained to idle gapers the folly of Kentish justice and them that administered it.)

"It's prodigious!"

"It's amazing!"

"Done without kindling!"

"Of a violent beauty!"

"Ferocious!"

"Fearful!"

"Thtrange . . . motht thtrange!" (This from Hotspur, who had a lisp.)

Naturally, great interest was got, and the landlord further goaded Mr. Treet into agreeing to provide a sample of "Lucifer's Smoke" in the parlor when he should be unstocked that night. It was typical of Mr. Treet's grand-heartedness that he never saw he was being put upon to attract custom to the inn when business was bad. Like all men of great talent (and I include all we Treets, though three are female), Mr. Treet could abide anything without taking offense—anything, that is, save contempt for what God had given him— viz, his genius.

But more than anything, I think Mr. Treet was feeling the joy that was in all our hearts on being freed from the sinister Stranger. His eyes shone. His head was high . . . and his feet, through the boards, performed a gentle, tiny jig. And to us who knew him, and loved him, and respected him, there was no doubt—his quiet smiles and powerful brow gave it away—that he was meditating something special . . . something, even for Mr. Thomas Treet, quite extraordinary.

· 2 ·

To PERFORM in the Eloquent Gentlewoman, I may say, was no distinction. A very ramshackle, creaky structure whose portly bedbugs, it was said, could be heard at dead of night, munching the flesh of snoozing guests. But never the landlord's . . . no bug would have demeaned itself so, for he stank of tallow and old fish. Which was doubly unwholesome in someone who gave himself genteel airs, changing his inn's name from the Shrew to the Queen of Spain to the Eloquent Gentlewoman. As if *that* improved it!

At six o'clock Mr. Treet was released and went directly to our wagon, where he closeted himself for two eventful hours while we remaining Treets mounted a guard against gapers, brain-pickers, and thieves. By eight o'clock all was prepared. Mr. Treet was situated to produce "Lucifer's Smoke."

But, owing to the landlord's being confident that he'd not yet got every capable drinker crammed into the parlor, we had to wait till a quarter after nine. All of us—even Hotspur, who was grown so sleepy, he kept falling off his stool in a doze.

By nine o'clock the parlor was objectionably full, and the landlord had a great quantity of watered ale stacked in a corner, knowing that smoke is a powerful provoker of thirst. We Treets sat about the table very soberly dressed . . . which always makes a good impression, like we were merchants of the House of Nature, traveling in her mysteries.

Of which "Lucifer's Smoke" is a striking sample. Oil of Sugar and Crystals of Violet are its principals . . . to which is added more remote substances—hard to come by—for to produce your true, purple-bellied, brooding fog of "Lucifer's Smoke." But, like all geniuses, Mr. Treet delights to experiment, changing the proportions of this and that for a more prodigious effect. Sometimes he fails—but sometimes he achieves effects that amaze even him . . . and he sits back and smiles at the rest of we Treets, entirely beyond words, while the phenomenon he's called into being roars and riots about his head like a storm of ghosts.

Just such a storm awaited the parlor of the Eloquent Gentlewoman.

At a quarter after nine to the minute Mr. Treet said, "Gentlemen and landlord—all I ask is that there shall be no panic." Laughter and jeers, at which he smiled patiently; then, when the vulgar uproar was done, went on with great gravity, "I beg of you—no movement about the room nor desperate attempts to escape, for there'll be no harm if you remain still. Do not grow fearful if curious and frightening shapes seem to be forming in the dense air. These are but the phenomena of Nature, not devils—though they may seem to be horned and malignant. Do not strike out at them—even if they seem to be engulfing you, for they are harmless, I promise you."

He brought out the crucible from under the skirts of his coat and placed it on the table. A very satisfying silence. All about us heads ancient and modern craned to observe the crucible's contents—two vital substances of which were still lacking.

Mr. Treet snapped his oiled fingers at Hotspur—then at me, the Alpha and Omega of the family, as he put it. Hotspur handed him one of the substances . . . and I gave up the last—the fateful Crystals of Violet.

Mr. Treet said, "I give you—'Lucifer's Smoke,'" and tipped first one and then the other into the crucible.

Thirty seconds is the breeding time of "Lucifer's Smoke"—thirty quiet, brooding seconds in which the tiny, peaceful souls of the substances in the crucible become aware of passionate love and enmity . . . seethe inwardly till the oppressive proximity of each other becomes too horrible to be borne. Thirty famous seconds in which the inhabitants of the small copper world prepare for the revolution and blazing war decreed by Nature and invoked by Mr. Treet.

I saw a man between the window and the door. Either he was perched on a bench or was amazingly tall, or else his frantically inquisitive head had broken loose from the mooring of his neck and floated up into the sweaty, beer-stained air. On his pocky face was a look of gratifying alarm and wonderment. . . .

"Twenty-seven . . . twenty-eight . . . twenty-nine . . ." tolled Edward, who, at twelve, was the most scholarly of we Treets, and destined to follow in Father's explosions.

". . . Thirty!" breathed the pocky giant between the window and the door—and the crucible went up in a soft, white bang!

Many times in my own memory Mr. Treet's made "Lucifer's Smoke," for Mr. Dymer's Company, and Mr. Robinson's Company—and once for some gentlemen from Bristol, but never had he surpassed his achievement in the humble parlor of the Eloquent Gentlewoman upon that November night.

At first the issuage was small and a light yellowish-brown—due to the Berlin Syrup of which Mr. Treet was very fond—but then it gathered strength. It seemed to hurry out of the crucible at a tremendous speed so that it made a short solid column, veined with fire, before the billows began to form and take on the invisible shapes of the air's currents. Then these billows, vaguely tinged with brown, purple, and even green, stood fat and bulky in the middle air before they was pushed and tumbled out of place and shape by urgent, thicker newcomers—like a crowd at a wedding or a hanging. . . .

Gasps, cries, even shouts of amazement filled the parlor—for the Eloquent Gentlewoman might suddenly have been in Tartary or Arabia or any other such marvelous place. The sweaty men of Kent, the conniving landlord, the dusky ceiling and the filthy walls—all was swallowed up in the oozy grandeur of "Lucifer's Smoke" . . . all save the mean tallows that, here and there, lit the underbellies of the clouds like the vague fires of cities burning on a plain. Yet there was no acridity nor sourness in the fog. This was Mr. Treet's greatest secret and partly due to the presence of pure Salts of Fire in the crucible.

Last to vanish had been my pocky giant by the wall— high up, his head cradled in vapors that kissed his chin, his open mouth, his old nose, then his wondering eyes (seeing God knows what marvels!), till naught was left but a greasy tuft of hair, growing up out of the vapors like a clump of reeds from a marsh mist.

Then we Treets, being accustomed to wonders, glanced to where we knew one another was with commonplace affection (being united in talent, so to speak) and began to beat the air with open hands to make still more remarkable shapes in the clouds.

This was a great joy—particularly to Hotspur, who fairly capered about (when one glimpsed him), making loops and spirals of cloud, and sometimes puffing—big-cheeked, like a wind angel on a map—lumbering argosies toward the window, the doors, and the privy.

And still the crucible foamed! Afterward, it was said, the air grew so dense that a mean Kentish thief picked his own pocket of seven pound and paid off two debts with it before he'd discovered what he'd done!

But there was something else that happened—something at once extraordinary and even terrifying. . . . The air was at its most crowded with mountains of light and color tumbling upon each other (like it must be in heaven) when they broke and swirled and stormed in a mad commotion! Furiously, they fell upon one another . . . colors dying into purple, gray—even black . . . till a long, dark funnel seemed to be roaring from the crucible to the night!

And then—and then, along this funnel, toward the vague shape of Mr. Treet, moved a darker shape . . . tall, with flapping blacknesses about its shoulders and head!

"What's that? . . ."

"It's gone cold as the grave!"

"What's he done?"

"Did you see it?"

"What? What?"

"The shape! Black! Horned! Corpse-faced!"

"He's called up the Devil!"

I heard Mr. Treet scrape back his chair—saw him rear up to his feet.

"So you've come!" he muttered.

The figure in black halted. An uncanny moment. Vapors swirled about his gray, dingy face . . . licked at his rheumy eyes.

"But will come no more, Mr. Thomas Treet. My Principal instructs me—come no more."

It was the Stranger—come like the Devil to a christening! He'd opened the door and let in the night, which had rushed across the parlor to the opened door opposite (left so by the landlord, who'd blocked the passage with too much ale) and so made the dark funnel in the smoke down which he'd walked.

For a moment our father stood speechless. Then I think someone—maybe it was the wind—shut one of the doors and the dark funnel began to fill up with "Lucifer's Smoke," so the Stranger became obscured till he was scarcely visible, and might have been a trick of the moving vapors . . . a shape that looked like a man, but was not.

"After thirteen years!" I heard Mr. Treet cry out, his voice much altered and unequal. "And *now* you say 'no more'! What must I do? Thirteen years is too long! May God have mercy on me, but I'll not continue! No! No! Let the fires of Hell come and scorch me! I've a soul, sir! Tell your Principal that! Did he think he'd bought me forever? Go tell your Principal that his 'no more' frees

Thomas Treet forever! 'No more' is as good as enough! Begone, you dingy devil, sir! I *will* not continue!"

But, grand as he'd been, Mr. Treet had been defying his own "Lucifer's Smoke," for the Stranger had gone directly, leaving the parlorful of boozers to conclude that our father had made a bargain with the Devil—and was trying to escape it. And, indeed, we Treets half thought so too . . . for Mr. Treet's pallor and gloomy trembling was something outside of our knowledge of him.

"Get out! Get out!" bawled the landlord, seeing a chance of saving on the supper and bed he might have been obliged to furnish for the entertainment. "I'll have no black magic in my inn! Never come back no more, devil-sent Treets! No more Novembers here, I say!"

Back in the wagon, our father answered not a word to all our questions. All he could manage was to shake his head, over and over again . . . then beg us not to wake Hotspur, for he'd howl.

He was sitting on the basket that contained our best linen and some of his profoundest secrets. I remember, he kept tugging at a piece of cane that had frayed and worked loose. He seemed almost angry with it. Then he fetched a deep, deep sigh and stood up.

"George . . . George, my dear—I must go outside, and think. . . . See that Hotspur don't wake up. And—and all of you, try to sleep."

He said this last with great gloom, as if sleep was a privilege henceforward denied him. Then he climbed outside and we watched him in the moonlight—a very forlorn genius indeed. We saw him stroll aimlessly across the quiet marketplace . . . stop by the empty stocks—whose leg holes looked like wide-awake eyes—then sit by that object of his shame, for all the world like a tired man enslaved by a glaring, watchful beast.

Which was amazing, for nothing could have seemed more wonderful than the Stranger's coming no more. All our lives we'd dreamed of a joy such as this! No more black Junes and Novembers! The sinister fellow had said so himself. Yet Mr. Treet was in a dump so deep, there seemed no coming out of it.

"It's the guineas," declared Rose Treet, whose genius—though she was but ten—was chiefly financial. "Our father's in the dumps on account of losing them."

"Then why was he in the dumps when he got them?" I asked. "There's more to it than money, Rose Treet."

Then Jane, who, in some ways, was most like our father, said if we went to sleep directly, the mystery would be solved in the morning when we'd all be fresh to consider it.

But Edward, the scholar Treet, thought otherwise.

"Thirteen years, our father said. That means none of us was here when it all began. Excepting you, George. And you was one year old. What happened, George, when you was one?"

"I can't remember."

"Try, George," went on Edward, encouragingly, for he considered himself to be hot on the scene of the mystery. "Think of cribs and cradles and bibs and bonnets. Don't anything come back to you?"

But though Edward was a scholarly and historical genius, he was a younger one than I, and I told him it was stupid to expect anybody to remember the first year of his life. Not even Hotspur or Henry could do that. (Both of them were fast asleep, so there was no chance of asking them. Besides, though their first year wasn't so far off, they could scarcely remember last year . . . and often forgot things more recent than that!)

Nonetheless, the reminder of "thirteen years" gave me an uncomfortable feeling that the Stranger was indeed somehow my concern . . . and I remembered his uncanny looks at me whenever he came.

There was a short silence in which Nell Treet joined Henry and Hotspur in a softly snoring sleep . . . making faint clinking sounds from time to time, as she turned over and over and her bracelet kept touching a jar. Our father was still outside.

"The clue to the mystery," said Edward, softly—for there was no stopping him thinking and talking about it—"is not why the Stranger came in the first place, but why he's not coming anymore."

"Good night, Edward."

"Good night, then, George."

I think it was close to two o'clock, and I was the last of the Treets awake. I climbed out of the wagon and went quickly to join my father. He started with alarm when he saw my shadow.

"I couldn't sleep."

"Why not, George?"

"The Stranger . . . his words . . . yours and your mood, sir."

He nodded, and, with bewilderment and dismay, I saw his eyes were filled with tears!

"Father! Mr. Treet, sir! What's wrong?"

"There's nothing wrong, George. Indeed, in a way . . . that is, from your point of view, everything's suddenly right!"

"How do you mean, sir?"

He blinked his eyes and ran his fingers along the

edge of the stocks . . . almost as if he was abruptly fond of them.

"George."

"Yes, Father?"

"Are you in good heart?"

"Yes, Father."

"And of strong spirit and high ambition?"

"Yes, of course, Father. For ain't I a Treet?"

"No, George. You are not. And the time has come for me to take you home. You are not my son. You are the child of a great nobleman . . . rich and mighty. You have another father—and a mother too. You have another name . . . and another world—which, with your genius and talent, will become a universe, my dear. . . ."

· 3 ·

MORNING—AND the Treets knew! They stared.
They gaped. They laughed; they were amazed. They
weren't surprised; they knew it all the time.

"It is *Lord* George?" "*Prince* George?" "*Duke* George?"
"*Baron* George?" "*Earl* George?" "*King* George?"
(This last from Hotspur, whose ambition knew no
bounds.)

"Quick! There's a crown in the basket! Put it on his
head! Off with his common hat! Give him the crown!"

"There's robes in the basket! Off with his poor old
suit! He must wear robes!"

"Will it be ten thousand a year, George?" asked Rose
Treet, deeply interested.

"What's your lineage, George? Back to the Conquest—
or before?"

"Will you go hunting?"

"Will you go to Court?"

"Will you thtill *fly*, George?" This from Hotspur—
and it caused me a small prick of regret, but not for long
. . . for the uproar in the wagon grew and grew—like

one of Mr. Treet's own magical concoctions—till it was impossible to think of anything save defending myself against the cheerful pinching and poking and hair-pulling of my one-time brothers and sisters. "For," said Jane Treet, "the next time we'll see him, we'll have to be more polite."

Naturally, I felt deeply sorry that the Treets should be losing me—but, when that wild and amazing scene had died down (for the Treets, though they had their genius, were not very genteel), I promised that they'd be seeing me often and that I'd be well situated to advance their genius, maybe on the London stage. At this Mr. Treet nodded strongly, and remarked that he was glad I'd grown up so generous and gentlemanlike under his instruction, and that I did credit to the name of Treet. Of which I never need be ashamed. Treet was a good name. Treet was a fine name. Treet was a name to conjure with . . . ha! ha!

My real name was Dexter. *George* Dexter? Hopes of something grander were crushed. George was indeed my name. Where did I come from? Sussex. Hadn't I noticed we were traveling in that direction?

Amazing! I'd thought we were going to the moon! For the passing landscape—which I'd seen many, many times before—seemed suddenly as strange as on another world! Hills and valleys seemed to've changed about—like I was standing on my head. . . .

I sat in my usual place, beside Mr. Treet, while the others crowded their heads through the opening in the canvas to hear what was being said.

Dreamily, and with many pauses when recollection failed, Mr. Treet related what had happened thirteen years ago, and, as he talked, vague memories (or memories of memories, I suppose) seemed to stir within me of another life. They were much clouded, as deep meaning swam under his narrative, like monsters hidden from sun and light.

In those far-off days Mr. Treet had been but a traveling conjuror—ambitious, but with no more to his credit than a handsome wife. It was in Sussex . . . a certain village . . . a certain inn . . . a place very often visited—till after that particular June. And then never no more for a good reason.

Between nine and ten o'clock in the evening . . . a most violent thunderstorm, so that the beating on the inn door was took at first for thunder. Then the door seemed to be burst open by a lightning bolt, and in the streaming blackness stood—the Stranger!

Without a word he elbowed his way into the parlor—elbowed, for his arms were incommoded, being filled with a child!

An extraordinary feeling gripped at my heart! Was it the long-forgotten memory of a dark and thunderous ride, fiercely clutched in thin, malignant arms against the lightning and the teeming rain?

"The child will die of wet and cold!" cried Mr. Treet, vastly concerned.

"Indeed?" said the Stranger in his papery-dry voice (which was the only dry thing about him, for he pooled water wherever he moved). "It wouldn't be a bad thing if he did! My Principal would not be distressed on that account!"

"Then your Principal must be the Devil himself!"

The Stranger smiled. ("And a vastly unpleasant thing it was," remembered Mr. Treet, shivering slightly.)

"Then take the child. Bring him up if you will—or drown him in the nearest river. My Principal won't object, I promise you! And, if you take him, my Principal will undertake to pay you thirty guineas every June and November. Always provided you keep away from this place—and out of Sussex. My Principal will insist on that. Is it a bargain?"

"What if I refuse?" asked Mr. Treet, not much inclined to do any such thing.

"Then I'll go elsewhere," said the Stranger grimly, "or bury this brat wherever he dies, for he'll not survive much longer in this stormy night!"

Then Mr. Treet went on to tell of the Stranger's subsequent visits . . . of how they were arranged, the third of each June and November—November in Faversham, June in Rye, till Faversham was changed to Sandwich. . . . Until now. And now, it seemed, the bargain was broke, and Mr. Treet's conscience shouted aloud for me to be returned.

"For we guessed where you was stolen from, George," he said. "The great house was not far from the inn— and you was not soaked enough to've come farther. We knew you was the only son of Sir John Dexter, my dear—but we loved you as if you were our own!"

This recital took a great part of our first day's journey toward Sussex, for it was not allowed to be told straight through. It was examined and questioned and exclaimed on at every twist and turn. Not by me—for I was deep in a dream of my amazing change of fortune—but by the six inquisitive Treets behind. At every point there was no less than six questions—often eight or nine, for Edward was so curious that one might have supposed he was bringing out a history of the Dexters in three volumes octavo, to be printed by September next! On the other hand, Rose could not conceal her disappoint-

ment that my father was but a baronet—indeed, she
scarcely tried!

"Of course I know that baronets can be as rich as
butter, George, but it ain't the same as being a lord."

Having started unnaturally early we'd had hopes of
reaching Ashford that evening, but we'd made slow
progress owing to Otway's seeming to take a part in the
conversation, by stopping and whinnying—like he sensed
there was a disturbing upheaval among his amazing and
well-loved family. So we got no farther than Canter-
bury. But on the next day he went like he'd offended
the Dean and Chapter and could scarce get out of Kent
quick enough, and clumped and steamed into Tenterden
an hour after nightfall.

The stocks there were occupied. I thought we'd seen
their resident before—and wondered if he could have
been our friend the highwayman, for he waved as we
passed by. . . . But it might only have been the effect
of the stocks themselves on him, creaking confidentially, "There goes a popular old tenant of mine!
Leasehold—with an option!"

The chief of the second day's home-going was spent
in good Mr. Treet's giving me best advice on how to
conduct myself as a nobleman's son. With much help
from the rear, for there wasn't a Treet who, at one time
or another, hadn't appeared before the public as a
specimen of something lofty and genteel.

"Be courteous, but not humble," advised Mr. Treet.

"You be overbearing, George!" shouted Hotspur.
"Great gentlemen ith alwayth overbearing. Ain't they?"

"Only fools are overbearing—"

"Everybody'th a fool who'th not a Treet!"

Two days ago I might have agreed with him. Today I
felt peeved—even offended—though Hotspur grinned

affectionately and was much bewildered when a sister urged restraint.

The third day saw us in Sussex itself and we stayed the night in Lewes. There had been a deal of mist about, and, in places, it assumed the proportions of a fog—half hiding a bony-looking landscape.

Thoughts of the Principal began to prick me . . . and why he should have broke the bargain. Vainly, I asked Mr. Treet. No answer. More than likely he never knew who the Principal was. Always dealt with the sour-faced intermediary. . . .

"An historical engima," said Edward. "That's what it is. For we must ask ourselves, why was you took, George?" He paused. "And why are you being brought back? That's an interesting question too—even though it's not historical. Maybe it's even more interesting than the first? Maybe—"

Mr. Treet told him to be quiet—and urged me to be content and accept my extraordinary change of fortune without questioning. Then, with a frown at Edward, he said:

"That's the gentlemanly thing to do."

Next day—the fourth and last of our journey—we began vastly early.

The road began to narrow, and seemed to be winding downhill. I say "seemed" for the thick vapors we'd noted yesterday were much in evidence, obscuring the prospect and clogging the hedgerows like clumps of wool from a giant's sheep. Mr. Treet said this part of Sussex was always mist-bound, lying, as it did, in an armpit of the Downs and collecting sea mists which were never dispersed.

Where were we? Coming toward a village called Fulking. Was it—*the* village? It was.

A heavy silence fell on the lumbering wagon—a very grievous silence as we approached my journey's end. Then we came to the inn—the Shepherd and Dog—and I stared at the parlor windows, vaguely troubled. . . .

"Treets," said their father, mournfully. "Here you must stay awhile, for George and me has business at the Manor."

So how does one part from six of the most talented personages in England, who'd become the furnishings of my life and dreams and deepest love? 'Tis a problem not easily overcome.

"It's a historic sadness, George," said Edward, gloomily.

"And a great loss," said Rose.

"We shall miss you, George," said Henry and Nell together, but not with much conviction—for I think they were too young to understand we were parting for more than a day or two. . . . I turned to Miss Jane Treet—a great lady and a great actress though she was but eleven.

"Good-bye, George Treet," she said sadly—then smiled and curtsied with a "Pleasure to make your acquaintance, George Dexter, Esquire! I hope we'll meet again!"

"Indeed we will! Oh indeed—indeed!"

And then I remembered Hotspur. Where was he? Fallen asleep in the wagon!

"For pity's sake don't wake him up! He'll be sure to howl! Hotspur Treet—the genius of sleep!"

At last Mr. Treet—who'd been engaged with the landlord for the hiring of a curricle to drive to the house in some sort of gentlemanly style—was ready. We mounted up, Mr. Treet deftly flicked the whip, and, almost directly, the line of waving Treets vanished as we took a sharp turn in the road.

"Mr. Treet?"

"Yes, George?"

"Do you know Sir John and Lady Dexter?"

"Only by hearsay, George," he answered, without taking his eyes off our trotter's mincing rump. "I understand Sir John to be a remarkably fine sort of nobleman . . . very gentlemanly in his dealings and careful of his good name."

"And—and Lady Dexter?"

"Somewhat prouder, I believe . . . for, when I was here before, she was never known much outside of the Manor. I heard once that she was something of a beauty, but if she was the lady I once saw driving by the church, then she was too pale for my taste—"

"But not for my father's!" I said sharply—and Mr. Treet sniffed and held his tongue.

Silence, for above three minutes.

"Mr. Treet?"

"Yes, George?"

"For the last time, sir—who is the Principal?"

Silence, for above half a minute.

"Never ask me that. Never. Nor ever speak of it in the house. Forget the Principal—and, God willing, he'll forget about you. Be excellent, be courteous, be loving, be gentlemanly—in a word, be a Treet. For whatever you was born, George, you've gleaned advantages. Use your genius . . . but not for too much inquiring. Gentlemen don't ask. Gentlemen either know—or keep genteelly ignorant—with a smile."

We passed through a copse of silver birches, delicately nodding in the veils of mist—like a congregation of long-dead nuns, withered while at their Matins. . . .

"I know this place. We are nearly arrived. Prepare yourself, George. . . ."

I did indeed prepare myself, but not for what we found. We arrived at Sir John Dexter's door to discover that he was similarly arrived at another—Death's!

· 4 ·

FOR GOD'S sake, don't think me a monster (even though I have red hair!) when I say I was not plunged instantly into an anguish of grief when I learned that my father was dying!

For consider—I'd not seen him since I was one. Mr. Treet had stood in his stead since then. I was shocked—even distressed . . . but, in all honesty, a strong sickness in Mr. Treet would, at that time, have distressed me far more. A breakage, say, in Miss Jane Treet's leg would have made me turn whiter than did the six-foot-long by six-foot-deep face of the footman who answered our knock on the old-fashioned door. (Did I remember this door with its heavy carving? Did I remember even the Manor itself, anciently humped on its stone terrace like a giant about whom trees have grown up while he sits and waits and dreams, smoking, maybe, twenty pipes from his curious chimneys . . . ?)

But at first sight of him, my heart contracted in a most violent manner. For we were ushered in directly . . . through some ten miles of rich, quiet rooms, stared down upon by painted saints and Dexters (for a long while I wondered what one ancient Dexter had done to be shot full of arrows, till I discovered him to be a St. Sebastian and no relation at all) while the sepulcher-faced gent who conducted us kept murmuring:

"He's still a-dying . . . but peacefully now. Dr. Newby gives him another day . . . but . . . ?"

So was we expected? No. This was an idea of his—of my father's—at once curious and even noble. For he loved life, and, feeling himself to be departing it, would have no caller turned away—not even mendicants or gypsies, even. "What was it like outside?" he always asked—and, from the varied answers, built up some sort of sensation in his ruined self of the moving air and landscape so soon to lie atop of him. . . .

The room was thick—oppressive . . . with a staleness no quantity of Spirits of Wine could conquer. He had many visitors already . . . maybe a dozen (the room was huge enough to accommodate them and still seem empty save for the piled-up couch on which he was propped), seated in deep chairs, stood by the window confidently looking out . . . or standing beside him looking uneasily down. Dr. Newby, still in his green caped coat, creaked across the floor like the ghost of an enormous grasshopper.

"Won't be long!" he mouthed—and indicated the couch and its occupant with an air of conspiracy—as if the flickering out of his life was a great secret shared by everyone save my father himself.

"Who—is—it?" (My father's voice!)

"A Mr. Thomas Treet and—and—"

The footman hesitated, for he'd only Mr. Treet's card, on which I was not mentioned.

"Glad—to—make—your—acquaintance, Mr. Treet. Though it'll—not—be for long . . . eh, Doctor? Not—long—now. But thank you—for coming, Mr. Treet. Pray—tell—me, sir—what is—it—like . . . outside? The autumn smells . . . are they—rich and heady, sir? Humor me and—and describe them. . . . But—but—*who's—that—with—you*, Mr. Treet? I—I cannot quite see him. . . . Pardon me . . . for not rising, sir . . . I—I'm indisposed, eh, Doctor? Humor me, Mr. Treet—you and—and your companion. . . . Stand in my sight, I beg . . ."

We moved nearer, and he went on talking—in a voice that was all but drowned by his own breathing . . . talking about this and that—the weather, country affairs, even the firmness of the ground underfoot . . . small things absorbed him much. Mr. Treet answered—as best he could, but was not much heeded. My father's eyes were upon me. . . .

Strange, profound eyes, exploring, from second to second, some absorbing mystery under his lids. His face was gray as stones, down which two or three streams of sweat ran in grooves they seemed to've worn. These same streams must have had their source somewhere in his faded red hair, for, wipe it as Dr. Newby might, his bony brow was never dry. And yet he was smiling.

"*Who—is—he,* Mr. Treet? Who—have—you—brought—to visit—me, sir?"

"I—I've brought back your son, Sir John. This is George Dexter—your son, sir!"

I understand there to've been some commotion in the room. A glass was dropped and a chair overturned with the noise of a coaching calamity.

"You've killed him!" mouthed Dr. Newby—glaring at

me with amazement and dislike—for my father's eyes had closed!

"Mr. Treet . . ." murmured my father, his face grown old and grim. "You—walk—upon—dangerous—ground. . . ."

"Scoundrel! Mountebank! Vagrant!" mouthed Dr. Newby—who'd grown so used to not letting his patients hear him, he'd all but lost the use of his voice.

"Sir John—I speak the truth! I do assure you, sir—he *is* George Dexter—I—I have proof, sir!"

Mr. Treet—a vastly uneasy Mr. Treet—fumbled in the skirts of his coat. What was coming? In a mounting panic I hoped it was "Lucifer's Smoke"! For I had an abrupt desire to vanish into something absolutely impenetrable! Things were taking an ill turn! Too many hostile eyes were scraping me raw. . . . Every person in the room (save one) was on his feet and closing in upon my dying father, Mr. Treet, and me.

"This shawl, sir; this linen, sir; these items of wool, sir . . ."

Mr. Treet had brought them out of his coat and, almost pleadingly, was holding them up for the closed eyes to see. As he did so, he related—with nervous haste—what he'd confided in me of the inn and the Stranger, of the making and breaking of the unnatural bargain (all in the self-same words), and, lastly, of the appalling force of his own conscience that had driven a coach and four through his heart and soul that night in Sandwich—through which painful hole he'd followed, wagon and children, in the morning—to this place.

"For—pity's—sake, Mr. Treet . . . don't torment me more!" (For pity's sake, Mr. Treet—let's be gone!)

Then something dropped from Mr. Treet's capacious pocket—something that gave a tiny ringing, rattling sound as it fell. I saw my father's eyelids—veined like

an autumn leaf—quiver. No one in the room spoke.
Save one.

"What is that?"

The voice came from by the window, from the one
seat still sat in, from the one person who'd not yet
moved. But now she did. Lady Dexter. Tall, with a face
cold as window glass from too much looking through it.
She rustled harshly across the room.

"What is that, sir?"

Dr. Newby bent and picked the object up. Handed it
to Lady Dexter.

"Ma'am . . . 'tis a child's rattle!" he mouthed.

A rattle. And I sensed my life depended on it! An
infant's rattle . . . shaped like a Harlequin's head. Made
of basketwork, with scratched blue and gold paint still
on it. A rattle that held a tiny gilt bell. An unusual rattle
. . . perhaps the only one of its kind.

Lady Dexter fingered it . . . tapped it . . . held it up
like a quizzing glass. Quizzed the room, turning sharply
from caller to caller . . . even to Mr. Treet (who red-
dened). But not to me.

Had my father's eyes drifted open? Or was he staring
through closed lids? The extreme bonyness of his face
seemed softened somewhat . . . as if—

A sharp, crackling sound! The rattle's handle—of old
cane—had snapped in Lady Dexter's whitened fingers.
She smiled—freezingly.

"Mr. Bennett!" (To one of the callers . . . a stout,
red-faced man with a churchly air.) "Do you think this
boy to be what he claims?"

Mr. Bennett came close. His breath smelled of Ma-
deira and old cheese.

"He has red hair. He—he comes with some credentials. We must not set our hearts against a miracle—"

"Fool! Fool!" Lady Dexter cut him off—and turned elsewhere. (Did a frown pass over my father's face? Or was it his cold wife's shadow?)

"Mr. Rumbold!" (Stouter than Mr. Bennett . . . and even redder, but not so churchly.) "Give an opinion, sir! Come—be honest! Could this boy be what he—what is claimed for him?"

"I think not, ma'am."

(Why did my heart drop like a plummet? God alone knows I'd no present ambition for this fierce lady to be my mother! And yet—my heart dropped!)

"Why? Why not, Mr. Rumbold? What's against him? Hasn't he red hair? Hasn't he *credentials*? This rattle." (She quizzed me briefly through it—and her eyes sparked like caged diamonds!) "It is *the* rattle, you know, Mr. Rumbold! Or do you think him too well grown for a Dexter? Too—shall we say—*ordinarily* amiable? Even too handsome, Mr. Rumbold?"

"No, ma'am. Not—er—elegant enough—"

"Is *that* all? Fool! Fool! What's elegance? *You* might have been elegant if you'd not been brought up in a stable! As it is, you've grown to resemble an ass! Don't talk to me of elegance!"

(Was my father smiling? If so—then he was alone in it. But then, dying grants some privileges.)

"Dr. Newby!"

The good doctor gave a leap of alarm.

"Ma'am?" (His voice—shook out of him—was oddly high and nervous.)

"Your opinion, sir?"

"Opinion, ma'am? I've no opinion."

"What? Not even a fool's?"

"Fools give opinions. *I know!*"

A feeling of sickness oppressed me—a horrible sickness, consequent on a conviction of failure and abrupt dismissal. (My father's face! Was the sweat swollen to a flood? Or was it because Dr. Newby had paused in wiping it away?)

Dr. Newby continued, "When George Dexter was an infant, I remember he was in the care—or lack of it—of a wretched nurse."

"I remember . . . I remember . . ."

"Then do you remember, ma'am, that she let him fall on the terrace?"

"I remember . . . I remember . . ."

"And he suffered an injury. A cut. Deep. Shaped like a comma. Over his right eyebrow—"

"Yes! I remember!"

(My hand went to my head!)

"Then look, ma'am. The scar! There's no doubt! This is George Dexter indeed!"

My father's face! He was smiling with the most extraordinary gentleness and triumph! But be quiet! He was talking! Softly . . . with much difficulty . . .

"Thank you, Mr. Treet . . . you—have—done—me—some service, sir . . . some—service . . . and you, Doctor . . ."

"So! You have come home then!"

Then from my mother no sound for a long while. Her eyes gazed steadily at me but they did not smile. She remained stiff and unyielding, as if all sensibility had been frozen out of her. Then, suddenly, she turned, almost violently, to another caller I'd not noticed—a caller who'd remained by the fire. A sickly-looking bundle in a cloud of black.

"Do you wonder why I never asked your opinion, madam?"

The bundle gave a smile as sickly as her complexion. And her head nodded.

"Because I knew what that opinion would have had to be. And what it would have been worth, Mrs. Montague!"

All this while she was pacing up and down, making a great commotion with her gray silk gown. Mrs. Montague had vainly tried to follow her with her eyes . . . then dropped them after one venomous flash at me. (Was she the Principal, I wondered, in a moment of strong alarm?)

"Well, Sir John"—my mother had paused by my father's couch—"it seems we have George back again! You must recover, sir! Your son needs a father as well as a mother!" Then she turned to speechless, tragic Mr. Treet. "Some sort of thanks to you. Yes—he does you credit, Mr. Treet."

"More, madam!" said Mr. Treet, in a sudden, glorious burst of pride. "He does *you* credit!"

They gave Mr. Treet a thousand pound before he left—as a stop for the hole his conscience had made in his heart and soul and family—and had the kindness to let him and me make our farewells alone.

"Well, George . . . a fine house, eh? Worthy people, my boy . . . noble, rich. Exactly as I told you."

"Yes, Mr. Treet. A great lady . . . my mother."

"Oh—you'll grow to love her, George. You have an affectionate nature."

"But has she, Mr. Treet?"

"Oh, undoubtedly! Not a doubt in the world!" (Maybe not in the world at large, but in my head a whole battalion!)

"Where are you going now, Mr. Treet? What will you do with your windfall, sir?"

He looked wistful—then brightened up remarkably.

"My old ambition you know, George. A London theater. A grand Scientific Affair. Myself and six Treets. Opportunity there! Oh, we'll make our names, my boy!"

"Will I not see you often, then?"

Here, Mr. Treet looked awkward and uncomfortable.

"Not at first, George. Not a good idea you know. For, in our different stations, we must grow a little apart, my dear. . . ."

All this took place in a small antechamber before the great hall, and would have gone on for some while longer, had not a footman come by ushering out the sickly-looking Mrs. Montague. She stopped as she saw me and stared with her coal-black eyes.

"You are not George Dexter! You *cannot* be! For I've been talking with him these past thirteen years! Oh! God help me! God help me. . . ."

The footman curtly ushered her on with:

"She's evil, Mr. George, sir! She's been filling her ladyship's head with talk from beyond the grave! With talk from an infant devil she swore was the spirit of George Dexter! Most likely they'll hang her now you're home, sir!"

· 5 ·

WHAT A homecoming—to this vast, tremendous, dark, rich mansion . . . with its uncounted rooms and quiet servants . . . its cold mistress—and its dying master!

My bedroom was in the front of the house and looked out onto the terrace and beyond, though the ever-present mists obscured any great view. Were the Treets still by the inn? Or were they rumbling and trundling to London with their thousand pound? I wished them well. Profoundly.

I climbed into my bed—which was spacious enough for seven—and prayed for my father's recovery. Then, among a hundred other things, I began to think of the magnificence to which I was heir. Had it not been for the company of geniuses, I might well have been squashed flat by it! But, however sublime the elegance into which I'd come, I was confident I'd do myself justice.

For example, my clothes. There'd been more than dusty robes and tattered horns in the Treets' baskets—

there'd been a green brocaded coat, white silk breeches, red-heeled shoes with buckles like suns, and silk stockings with gold thread wove into the clock, called "bas de soye shot through." There was also a collar of Colbertine lace, and a waistcoat of silver lace mounted on yellow watered tabby (which Edward and John had once fought over). . . .

So you see, my appearance had been something of a gentleman . . . and I believed it to've met with some pleased surprise. My mother had not been able to take her eyes off me. Mr. Bennett had smiled. And even the servants, used as they were to gentility, had blinked. . . .

But I knew there was more to it than that. As Mr. Treet always said, "Clothes—though they might make the man—don't entirely make the gentleman. No, sir! No indeed!"

When he walks from room to room, he walks like there was a lady on his arm. At table, he don't spit in his glass to prevent his neighbor stealing. When he meets a servant, he don't elbow him aside, but greets him by name—if he knows it—and sets him at his ease with a smile. . . . And, if he should find himself in the kitchens, he don't go like a pig to the game pie without so much as a "by your leave, ma'am," to the cook first. He bows, and bids those present to take no notice of him . . . and, if they do, why, then he tells them tales—in refined words—of his adventures in a fantastic wagon (more of a coach, really) with a company of geniuses. (From the very first, I was vastly popular with the servants.)

And still there's more to being a gentleman . . . On my second morning, my mother asked:

"Did you sleep well, George?"

"Handsomely well, Mother."

"George . . ."

"Yes; Mother?"

"Now you've made yourself known to the household, there's no further occasion to spend all your time in the kitchens, eating and gossiping like a constable of the watch!"

An hour! That's all it had been! How could she have said it was all of my time? Had she forgotten my walks through the hall and library? My courtesies to Mr. Bennett and Mr. Rumbold? My shaking hands with Dr. Newby and my visits to my father to see if he was awake and would smile?

"And George . . ."

What else was coming? How else had I failed? I'd been good enough for the Treets . . . and they for me!

I fancy I frowned, for she saw that I was offended and said, suddenly, that there was nothing more—absolutely nothing! But it was plain there *was* something more. So I asked.

" 'Tis nothing much at all! Believe me, George, you've done nothing ill—even, maybe, a trifle too well? Though I wondered, George, if you had plainer clothes for every day? For 'twould be a crime to ruin such elegance with too much wear!"

(Did she consider me overdressed, then?)

"But no matter today, George. For we've to visit the Rumbolds—and 'tis suitable for you to look so—so splendid!

I breathed a sigh of relief. A further piece of mortification would have been too much!

Then, while my mother was making herself ready (for, she'd said, if I was going like a Prince, she'd feel ill at ease looking less than a Queen!), I occupied myself with studying the family portraits to pick up some hints on attitude and expression therein displayed. For I considered I ought to own some family mannerisms. . . . (A gentleman of Tudor times took my fancy, and I mastered the raised eyebrow and left hand lightly on hip tolerably well.)

But there was one thing that caught my attention . . . and was, in a queer way, chilling. In the library one of the picture frames was empty. Why? What had happened to the painting that had been in it? And of whom had it been? As I stared up at that empty place—whose very vacancy seemed particular by being enclosed—the feeling of coldness grew strong—as if there was cold air blowing out of the untenanted frame itself. . . .

The visit to the Rumbolds went off capitally. They were honored and delighted we'd called . . . for Lady Dexter had paid no visits since my father had been struck down. This was her first—and with her son.

My appearance, I was pleased to see, caused some admiration, Mr. Rumbold murmuring to his wife, "What did I tell you, ma'am? Didn't I speak the truth?"

"And what did you tell Mrs. Rumbold, sir?" asked my mother with her cold smile.

"That your son was come back—and—and what a fine fellow he was, ma'am," answered Mrs. Rumbold, quickly. "That's all he told me, your ladyship."

My mother nodded—and the conversation shifted to general country matters, with genteel inquiries as to how my father did. For some reason or other, I sensed my mother was not at her ease—and put it down to the strong smell of dogs and stables that filled the house. She kept glancing sharply from Mr. Rumbold to Mrs. Rumbold and to the several Rumbold children who kept darting into the room, staring, giggling, and running out. One of these—a short, fat female of about eleven, who looked exactly like a spaniel—stayed longer than the rest. She came in, perched on a chair, and stared at me with a face that grew redder and redder till I thought it would burst. Then she cried, "Oh, Mama! Papa was right! Ain't he the *thing*!"

Then she buried her face in her hands—and fled.

And then—of a vastly uncomfortable sudden—I understood that, to these dog-infested bumpkins, I looked ridiculous!

For myself, I didn't hugely care . . . for they looked ridiculous to me. But my mother was pale and trembling with shame on my behalf! Which was horrible! For that elegant lady must have been wishing herself and her overdressed son at the bottom of the sea, rather than endure the obliging sneers of her neighbors!

I felt myself go as red as the child who'd just fled, which hadn't happened to me since a long-forgot disaster on the stage. I looked to my mother—and attempted to smile reassuringly. To my deep mortification she turned away. God knew how much I'd offended her! I sensed the Rumbolds were enjoying it hugely. To blazes with them!

I got to my feet (and trod on the paw of one of their bad-smelling dogs, which yelped and screamed like I'd murdered it).

"This coat," I said, in high indignation, "that you plainly think comical, was worn by King Charles on his way to the scaffold! And these shoes and stockings by a Marshal of France! This waistcoat"—here, I flung open my coat so's they could see the better—"graced Othello of Venice and the Duke of Vienna. And my collar was worn by a Prince in the Tower!"

"George!" cried my mother, in alarm.

But there was no stopping me now. Too many memories of those great personages seized hold of me, and I began to walk about the room fairly filled with them!

Fragments of speeches came into my mind: farewells, soliloquies, grand defiance, humble regret . . . moving speeches, fiery speeches, profound speeches . . . speeches that would have drawn tears from stones! Mrs. Rumbold, I was cheered to see, was crying like a baby. Mr. Rumbold had his mouth open, and several little Rumbolds had crept in at the door and were sat in a silent, amazed row. Mr. Treet would have been proud of me.

" 'I kissed thee ere I killed thee, no other way but this,
Killing myself, to die upon a kiss.' "

I cried, seized up a fruit knife, and plunged it, seemingly, into my breast.

"No! No!" shrieked Mrs. Rumbold, as I staggered and sank with a sigh to my knees.

She was conquered. Mr. Rumbold was conquered—and the little Rumbolds were entranced. I glanced to my mother. Her lips were compressed—and her eyes turned down. For God's sake, which side was she on? Then she looked at me—and almost smiled.

"Oh, ma'am!" cried Mrs. Rumbold, when I'd assured her I wasn't mortally dead. "What a fellow you have! If you'll forgive me—there's never been a Dexter like him!"

"No indeed," said my mother, coolly. "I don't suppose there has."

We left soon after, despite the little Rumbolds' entreaties for a second performance, and, in the carriage, I ventured to look at my mother and grin. She did not return it. She said:

"You will never do that again. *Never*—d'you hear? Nor do I ever wish to see you in those clothes again!"

Then, seeing I was startled and dismayed, she laid her hand on my arm and added, more gently:

"I speak but for your own good, George, my son. Believe me—I do indeed! *For your own good.*"

Being much distracted I could not, at that time, take her harsh remark as proceeding from anything deeper than her old capriciousness of temper, which I hoped (and later began to suspect) contrary to her own true nature. . . .

When we reached our house, thank God, we were greeted with good news. My father had taken some hot meat broth, and it seemed that Death, not liking the taste, had retired a little way off. . . . But splendid as was this turn, it never deflected my mother from her sworn object. Almost directly she had the house scoured for clothes that would fit me in place of the ones to which she'd taken such strong objection.

That evening, somewhat sadly, I folded away my fine coat and waistcoat, my breeches and stockings, and laid them in a chest in my room. But not forever, I swore. Out they'd come when times would be gayer—and more in keeping with their mood.

· 6 ·

HE DID not die that day, or the next, or the day after that, and Dr. Newby was silently confounded.

He slept a great deal and, when he was awake, seemed to take comfort from gazing at me in my quiet, new clothes. My seat was put by his couch, and strangers, who might have distracted him, were no longer so readily admitted. For Dr. Newby allowed that he might now survive till Christmas.

This news was got out of him with some difficulty, owing to the doctor's habit of mouthing everything, so that the word "Christmas" came out like a nervous twitch.

"For God's sake!" exclaimed my mother. "Speak aloud, Dr. Newby! Sir John knows his own condition, sir! So whom are you hiding it from?"

Dr. Newby looked as shocked as if his pocket had been picked in church—for there's none so devoutly possessive as a physician with a sick man. . . . Nonetheless, he was prevailed upon to give his news, for my father had fallen asleep. He even agreed that the return

of his son might have assisted his own efforts to save my
father's life. For, though we were not to hope for his
recovery—for nothing less than a miracle could accomplish that (here Dr. Newby did his best to look like
such a miracle)—it happened sometimes that, even in a
darkening life, there was some sort of brightness—a
sunset, so to speak—at its close.

This new view of my situation in the house served
only to alarm and depress me . . . so's I must have
looked more like a sun that had set for some time—for
the doctor moved over to my side and put his arm
round my neck like I was a bottle of Holland physic!

"You must be cheerful—and smile, George Dexter!
My arts are powerless without your help! You must
never let him see your distress. For he lives in you,
George. Rather let him see that his son is joyful to be
home at last! Let him see you—on fine days—ride out
across the park. Let him see you, gentle and strong, at
your mother's side. Let him see all these things—and
more, if you can devise them—and then, maybe, his
evening will be longer than we now dare hope? For,
though Death's made a shrewd hole in him, we may yet
plug it awhile!"

He let go of my neck very gently—as if to see if all its
bones were present—and shifted over to my father's
side. He stared down frowningly, and fingered an oddly
sinister object that lay on a table at my father's head, an
object to which my father's eyes always strayed, from
time to time, with an expression of unearthly grimness
and even despair.

Then Dr. Newby looked inquiringly to my mother.
She shrugged her shoulders and nodded.

"He must know sooner or later, Dr. Newby."

I waited uneasily, wondering what was to come.

Not twenty days ago Sir John had left for London most mysteriously, and in some withdrawn dread. A well man? Hmm! As well as ever he *could* be. (Dr. Newby looked extraordinarily proprietarial at this.) He'd left upon a Tuesday morning. He, Dr. Newby, had thought there was no immediate danger to Sir John—though he misliked any autumnal traveling on account of the fog. And then came the Wednesday. Maybe an hour past midnight. Wretched weather. An unhealthy congregation of mist and fog, low-lying, so that, from any eminence, the trees looked like driftwood on a thick, gray, noisome sea.

A violent banging on the doctor's door—fit to waken the dead. (Though this was Dr. Newby's own expression, he frowned at it, like it was a piece of pig ignorance.)

"Who's there?"

"Joseph! From the Manor! For God's sake, come at once, sir!"

"Why?"

"Sir John! He's dead!"

"Then go fetch Mr. Bennett from the church! Dead men are out of *my* keeping!"

But it turned out he was quite dead. His coach had just returned from London. The door had been opened and Sir John—his white face swinging like the moon through cloud—had toppled out of the darkness and fallen to the ground.

"Consider the confusion," went on Dr. Newby, calmly. "Doubtless, many things were done that marred his chances. But at least someone"—he bowed to my mother—"had the wisdom to dispatch at once for me. And, when I came, I found him in this room with Death—the great Enemy—sitting in his eyes like he'd already taken up residence on a foreclosure.

"But stay! Life was still flickering! He whispered, 'My side . . . my side . . .' Hm! Unexpected, that. Cautiously, I began to examine. And what did I find? Blood! Blood, sir!

"Close on a pint I estimated, not including what must have been still on the carriage seat and floor. His coat had sopped it up and was strong with it. Also his waistcoat and linen. I investigated. Tenderly, you understand . . . for one may do much damage unwittingly. And so at last I came to his flesh. Pardon if I offend any stomachs, but Sir John's stomach was more offended. Or, rather, his left side, mercifully below his heart . . . yet injuring a lung, I fancied, and rupturing much muscle. What had offended it? This, Master George. Just this!"

He picked up the object on the table that had so fascinated my father. It was a piece of lead, much roughened, much dented, much raked by powder and barrel.

"He had been shot, Master George, most murderously—"

"Who? Who did it?" I cried in amazement and vague horror. But my father's eyelids were quivering, and Dr. Newby raised his finger to his lips.

"Another time!" he mouthed. "Not now!"

I cannot abide suspense. I grow very restless under it, and my hands—in particular—sweat a good deal, which makes them pick up dust and grit so's against anything light they look frighteningly black. I did what I could to hide them behind my back, for my mother (maybe following Dr. Newby's suggestion) had taken it into her head to walk me through the ground floor of the house. Abruptly she pointed out this and that treasure and valuable item—almost as if daring me to exclaim in wonder and so betray my thirteen humble years away. But, with my hands clasped firmly behind me, I walked beside her in an absorbed silence, thinking only of who could have shot my father.

The house, as I've said, was enormous—but so were my thoughts—and it seemed as though we walked for hours and never passed the same wonder twice: great chimney pieces carved by Mr. Gibbons, faded tapestries woven by doleful Crusaders' ladies—most likely in the very rooms in which they hung . . . rooms with deep, old windows, where the light, once inside, seemed to fumble for a way out . . . and the mists seemed to've penetrated, so's no vista of rooms emptying into rooms was ever quite clear, but retained a vague, withdrawn look, and had a curious smell of iron. . . .

Nothing signified . . . for nothing was as large as the little dented piece of lead in my father's room. . . . My mother rustled on—and I, hands still behind me, walked silent beside her—or maybe half a pace behind . . . for she kept glancing back to see if I attended. . . .

Once, she half offered me her arm, but she was wearing pale gray, and my hand would have looked like a great black spider on it. I fancied she was a trifle mortified by my not complying, so I hastened to smile and say, "Vastly elegant" to everything she pointed out. Even to the paintings of old Dexters—though God alone knows they were a corpse-eyed crew, who seemed not so much painted as grandly buried in their frames . . . as if, on the instant of death, they'd been hoisted up on the wall, ironed flat, and varnished against further corruption and decay.

"Vastly elegant," I said, then realized, with awkward dismay, I was looking at the empty frame in the library, that frame from whose odd vacancy a cold air seemed to blow.

There was a deep silence—in which, I suspected, my mother was digesting how closely she'd been attended to. Her lips were pressed tight together, and her pale cheeks were under attack from a flush.

"I—I meant the frame, ma'am . . . 'tis very elegant! But—but why empty? Was the painting damaged?" (I was aiming to recover the situation and make amends, but somehow failing slightly . . . for my mother was staring from me to the queerly empty frame with a dark expression.) "And—and who was it of? A Dexter or a Saint? Ha—ha!"

She widened her eyes, then said evenly:

"It was of the gentleman who shot your father. An uncle of yours. Richard. Captain Richard Dexter. Your father's brother." She paused, then added grimly, "*Vastly* elegant, ain't it!"

She left me—with my hands still fixed behind my back like they were glued there! I stared up at the vacant frame with unbelieving horror! Brother murdering brother? My blood began to prickle in my veins. Brother murdering brother! Cain and Abel. An ancient family indeed. Even Edward Treet would have granted that! Why had it happened? What the hatred? What the cause? Wildly, I searched my mind, but could find nothing. No cause in the world for such a crime. Outside of the Play. Kings murdered their brothers—but we were not kings. Yet it had happened—and the murderer's painted face had been ripped from its seating so's nothing of him might ever again be seen. Where was he now? Still alive—or hanged? No! They wouldn't hang a Dexter! Something grander for one of us! The block.

Dawn in the Tower. Drums. A shirt-sleeved figure between black executioners. Walking the last walk—his terrible but noble face bowed. The block. The ax. Then the end.

With a shock I conceived I was taking something of a gloomy pride in this blood-boltered family tragedy—even thinking of telling Edward Treet for his three-volume history. . . . Till, with another, darker shock, I realized more deeply that this was no mad, lurid King murdering his plotting brother. This was my own uncle, who'd shot to kill my own father!

"Oh my God!" I whispered. . . . "Why? Why?"

I did not have long to wait. Black deeds, once shown, seem to parade themselves thereafter. And even to have champions. I'd been observed—standing bewildered and fearful before the evil frame—by a certain footman: Joseph. A very odd person . . . not so much sinister as a humble admirer of that disagreeable thing. I never heard him approach—for he always walked quietly. (Sometimes, I wondered if he touched the ground at all.) I supposed he must have been standing behind me for close on a minute . . . most likely gauging the aptness of my mood, for he'd a good black tale to tell—and much enjoyed the telling of it.

"Mr. George, sir," he began—and I nearly leaped out of my skin! "Beg pardon for startling—but Mr. George, sir, I couldn't help seeing you was interested in . . ." He pointed to the frame. I nodded, helplessly, so, without more ado, he began.

There was an entail in the family, he said. Did I know what that was? (Begging my pardon, but, though I was a Dexter by birth, upbringing must have clouded my understanding.)

It was not an hereditary sickness . . . though it had

given rise to one. He, Joseph, believed there had been many such dark passages in the family's history on account of the entail. Not that the entail was an evil thing in itself—any more than the pretty, deadly nightshade was murderous—but it gave rise to evil thoughts and deeds in souls already inclined that way. Yet the entail in itself was noble and just. It declared that the Dexter fortune and estate belonged only to a Dexter—and one who'd always been a Dexter . . . not some flimsy female of the line who'd change her name by marriage. Nor to the widow of a dead Dexter—but to a male child. ("Such a male child was you, Mr. George, sir—and long may you live and avoid disaster.")

No others had survived of Sir John's marriage. Three had come into the world, only to perish within the week of entering it.

But, at last, one did survive ("Your good self, Mr. George," sir"), to the relief and joy of Sir John and her ladyship. But relief and joy being, as it were, morning sunshine on one half of the world of Dexter, they cast a black midnight on the other, younger half!

"Captain Richard Dexter—your uncle, Mr. George, sir—the younger brother, married to a buxom slut—alas, your aunt, Mr. George, sir—what had produced healthy male child after healthy male child by way of a reproach it seemed, *his* hopes were blasted, *his* brood, so hopeful of riches, was disinherited by your mewing, crying self. For you was a sickly babe at the outset, Mr. George, sir—and stand now of a healthful miracle, worthy of your name, which means 'Right.' "

Here Joseph paused, stroked his smooth face, and glanced up at the empty frame as if an invisible semblance of Captain Richard Dexter was crouched there, glaring bloodily down. And I, too, stared at that emptiness, shivering under the now icy chill that seemed to be blowing from it. For I understood—with the most horrible sensation in the world—that *I'd* been the cause of the murderous disaster! My own existence had furnished the necessary hate!

"Then it was him . . . ?" I whispered, and Joseph went on to conjecture how greed, hate, and fear had worked in the Captain's breast at the sight of me, till, shrinking from outright murder (for, when young, he was as much a weakling as a monster), he procured that abduction that nearly killed her ladyship and Sir John. So it was he who'd been the Principal!

"I was a gardener's boy at the time," continued Joseph, as if it was the most extraordinary and sinister thing to've been, "and never heard the full commotion. But I understand that Mrs. Smith—your neglectful nurse—fled for her life, and that, for a long while, Sir John believed you to've been taken by gypsies, for he refused to credit his own brother with so vile an act—him being a Dexter.

"And it wasn't till Mr. Craddock—your father's attorney, Mr. George, sir—heard certain unwise mentions made among certain disreputable officers of Captain Dexter's regiment that the truth came to be generally suspected. Though there was never any proof of it. Vainly, Mr. Craddock pleaded with Captain Dexter—for Sir John would never see him more—and vainly searches was made. Nothing . . . nothing . . . nothing."

Joseph paused—as if to let me savor to the full that Devil's Pudding which was the Dexter family affairs.

"But matters came to their terrible head just on a month ago. Mr. Craddock came to visit Sir John. It seemed something had been discovered about yourself . . . maybe only that you was still alive. Sir John was beside himself with passion and excitement. Abandoning all his old resolve, he went to London to plead with his brother. I understand he *knelt* before him in company! And for a man as grand and noble as Sir John— *that* was something, Mr. George, sir!

"The Captain denied all. Maybe, even laughed. Sir John, swallowing his pride, pleaded again! Still no answer. Sir John grew pale as death! Rage consumed him! Rage at the vileness of his own flesh and blood! Rage at the cruel, contemptible act of thirteen years ago! Rage at everything concerning the monstrous Captain Dexter! All poured out of him in high, dark eloquence! To which the Captain responded—under some influence of drink and bad acquaintance—with challenging his brother to a duel! A murderous thing to do—his being a soldier and horribly familiar with weapons! Sir John came back, put his affairs in order—then went off to be murdered.

"So your father's a-dying on your account, Mr. George, sir, and you should be proud! It's not every lad of fourteen who has some of the noblest blood in England dribbled on a carriage floor for him! Yes—you do well to look up at the empty frame in anger! Oh! God help Captain Dexter when you lays hands on him, Mr. George, sir!"

So it seemed I'd fallen heir to more than a great name and rich possessions. Among the splendid bric-a-brac was that dark trifle—revenge! If not dead, where was my uncle now? Broodily, I stalked the house with black thoughts for company. Revenge. The weight was terrible . . . even suffocating. Once, I caught sight of myself in a mirror and—after the initial shock (for it was dark and I'd been thinking on murders)—I realized I'd never have known myself, supposing I'd passed myself in the street. I'd have shuddered and wondered who was that drawn-browed and gloomy youth who looked like all the world was on his shoulders?

This dismal state lasted for about two days, and then, when no ghosts appeared, or messages were pushed under my door, or deadly whispers poked into my ear, I began to recover—and hope that Captain Richard Dexter had fled for his life to the other side of the world.

Little by little, my spirits began to return, and I renewed my efforts to dispense them in just proportion to my new situation—for what would have made the Treets laugh would have made the Dexters weep. Above all, a gentleman has a sense of fitness and knows these things. . . . God help him!

Oh! Mr. Treet! Could not your conscience have dozed awhile longer? Though honesty may be the best policy—surely there're some things that take precedence over mere policy? If only the money hadn't stopped!

· 7 ·

DECEMBER FIVE and three weeks a Dexter! No mean achievement, that. All my doubts, fears, alarms—together with much strangeness and awkwardness—had worn away. Rooms, stairs, doors, and aspects that had seemed as rich and remarkable as Indian marvels were already becoming familiar, and I could go from my bedroom to the kitchens, to my mother's parlor, to the orangery without losing my way above once or twice and finding myself confronted by a door I'd never before seen. (What was behind it? Mysteries . . . mysteries . . .) Servants, too, became more everyday—as every day I saw them—and consequently I began to grow used to their various and particular hauntings, for they came and went like genteel ghosts, smiling most politely, even through the woodwork. . . .

Even the gloomy distraction of a murderous uncle became almost a commonplace of life in the Manor; and the vacant frame in the library—though it still exercised my mind—did not do so as violently as before.

The respect of neighbors and the deference of tradesmen was another, more amiable, aspect of my new life, and one to which I took fluently. It proved a great consolation whenever I missed the Treets. Everyone seemed pleased, even honored to see me . . . and never gave me cause to doubt them. I fancy there's a great deal of nonsense talked about the loneliness of situation and riches, and the man who finds himself solitary with them would be even more so without them. As for the fears and worries they bring . . . well, indeed, I'd rather be distracted as to what to do *with* a thousand pound than wretched over being without it! For, after all, a rich man may always make himself poor if he chooses, whereas a poor man don't have that choice. (Talking of a thousand pound—what was going on in London these days? What grand production was being prepared? What new marvels from the Treets, God bless them?)

Two further qualifications remained for being a gilt-edged, brass-bound, coach-built Dexter. A mother who was cold, curt, ironical, inquisitive, and always surprising. Which I had. And a father, handsome in sickness, gentle, cheerful, pleased to see me, proud of my appearance, and rejoicing in my company. Which I had also.

"I would like," said he, one day when he was feeling talkative, "to've taken you hunting, boy. But alas! I'm incommoded! But, maybe someday, we'll shoot in the coverts? Are you good with a gun, boy?"

" 'Tis a family accomplishment," remarked my mother, coldly.

My father sighed, and reached out his hand to mine— almost touching it, but not quite. I made a move to oblige him, but he withdrew his hand to fiddle with his throat.

"Your mother's for softer pursuits I fear, boy. For she's a gentle lady," he added, somewhat incredibly.

On which, conceiving he hoped for the support of a son, I said, "I have some quality with weapons, sir. Mr. Treet was not neglectful."

"Ha!" said he, with a mischievous smile at my mother, who looked discomfited. "And what arms are you proficient with, boy?"

I'd not been boasting. My genius for the stage had required and got some excellence in every valiant implement that had come Mr. Treet's way.

"With musket, pistol, arquebus, blunderbuss, fowling piece, carbine, poniard, rapier, short sword, broad sword, dagger, and mace, sir!" I answered coolly and was annoyed to hear my mother laugh.

" 'Tis a compendium of hostility, Sir John! You should be proud!"

But my father had turned away and closed his eyes. So that remarkable, dominant lady crossed the room and laid her hand almost gently on my shoulder and murmured ironically:

"Dear George! Did Mr. Treet not teach you to shoot with a longbow and arrow? For I'd not wish you to be at a disadvantage!"

Then her face went cold as stone and she rustled abruptly away.

Even after that my father never spoke of my life with the Treets, for, I fancy, he was unwilling to give my mother the opportunity for displaying further scorn. Instead, he talked of where we might ride together—if he was ever well enough—and whom we might visit. He talked, even, of giving a ball at Christmas, when I might meet the neighborhood under the most prosperous circumstances. ("Do you dance,

George?" asked my mother, slyly. I nodded—but did not risk a reply.)

We became, in short, as good friends as his condition allowed . . . and, I believed, there grew between us a deeper secretive warmth that seemed to thrive in the chilly air of Lady Dexter's presence, as if prospering in disapproval. I regretted bitterly that I'd not known my father in his healthier days, for his amiable nature and fine gentlemanliness would have made for a splendid companion. And that he felt likewise I'd no doubt at all.

Till December five—and then a certain piece of news reached the Manor that had an extraordinary effect on him.

Captain Richard Dexter was in Newgate! He'd been arrested, tried, and sentenced to two years in that shameful place! The duel had been witnessed by a constable who'd straightway given evidence and the Captain had been taken at his lodgings. His wife and three children had gone with him to Newgate—not out of loyalty, but because they'd not a penny to bless themselves with, even supposing they'd been that way inclined!

This news Joseph passed on to me with much the air of an evil genius fallen upon hard times . . . for there was a threadbare air about him, as if his blandness was wearing thin.

"And that's not the worst of it," he said, after he'd related the above. "The worst, none of us dares to tell him" —meaning my father—"for it would kill him stone dead! And that's for certain, Mr. George, sir! For I was in the room when this least of the news was told by someone from Mr. Craddock's office. Great tears stood in your father's eyes at the shame of it! A Dexter, lodged like a felon! I think if they'd hanged the Captain he'd have been less distressed . . . for that would have been an end of it. I mean, Mr. George, sir—you can live down a death, but a life's always there to plague you!"

Joseph softly rattled on in this grimly philosophic vein, spicing it with references to Sir John's state . . . his pallor, his anger, his bitter dignity . . . his hopes for his son. . . .

While I felt a great flood of relief! And tried to conceal it from Joseph. Vengeance was out of my hands! For the first time in my life I was grateful to the law and obliged to a Justice! The monster had been confined. Which cheerful event, now being known, supplied the answer to nosy Edward Treet's great mystery, viz. "Why had I been returned? Why had the money stopped?" The reason was all too plain. There'd been no more money to send—because the sender was fixed in gaol!

How he must have sweated with rage and bitterness over the outcome of the duel! Not to've quite killed his brother—and to've quite ruined himself! All of thirteen years' careful cunning—thrown away! He must have tormented himself half to death as he lay in gaol, counting, maybe, the very hours to the uttermost extinction of his hopes. "Now he'll be approaching . . . now he'll be within . . . now he'll be recognized! The damned, damned Dexter!" He must have cursed himself for that fatal weakness of thirteen years before when he might have dashed out the infant's brains and did not! His wretched wife, his futile sons—smothering him like sodden curses, sent by Hell as a punishment for evil incompletely done! His black soul screaming, "Is it too late? Even now?"

*   *   *

"And so if you should see this man, Mr. George, sir . . ." Joseph was still murmuring on . . . about God knew what, for I'd gone off into a dream of dictating the above fearful events to an open-mouthed Edward Treet.

From which I awoke with a shock! Joseph was holding out a ragged-edged portrait that had been cut from its frame! A sallow face, seedily plump, looked up at me. A youngish face, with light blue eyes and a discontented mouth—yet with the hint of a smile, as if that discontent was provoking inward amusement of a none too wholesome kind.

"The likeness was took about the time *you* was took, Mr. George, sir. It's Captain Richard."

"And—and how should I see him, then?"

"Why—as I've been telling you, Mr. George, sir . . . the worst of the news! The murderous gentleman's escaped!"

My father was in a chair—and dressed. At first I'd thought he was gone—the couch was empty and the grand chair filled with a tremendous stranger. I'd never seen him dressed before: plum velvet with gold facings, very little lace, but that of a fine quality, and a Dutch wig that made him severely handsome. Sir John Dexter.

"You're late, boy. Where have you been?"

His voice had an edge to it, and his eyes had a chill. Which penetrated.

"About the house, sir . . . nowhere else. . . ."

Dr. Newby, who was present, mouthed something at me—but I was too distracted to take it in.

"Come here. Stand close to me, boy."

Three weeks a Dexter. I began to have serious doubts about the fourth. I walked to the chair. Stood beside it. Was inspected.

"What d'you think of him, madam? Does he not look like the nephew of a felon?"

I braced myself for some freezing answer from my mother. A vastly unpleasant morning—even though the sun was shining and there was scarce a mist to hide the gracious park.

My mother said, "I've seen more ill-favored youths, Sir John—"

"Where? Where?"

"In houses as noble as this!"

An unexpected ally! But an uncomfortable one, for I never knew with this ironical lady whose side she was on, or for how long. My father continued to stare at me.

"His complexion, madam. Is it not coarse?"

" 'Tis the effect of too much air. A little longer in this house and—and he'll be as pale as the best of us."

"Your father's had bad news, George," said Dr. Newby, driven into outright speech. "Vastly unsettling news."

"I know."

"Gossiping with the servants?" said my father—then, quite suddenly, seemed to repent of his harshness and smiled rather sadly, I thought. . . .

I wondered wildly whether I ought to burst out with a host of tormented questions concerning my monstrous uncle—heartfelt questions, passionate questions, angry questions, questions that betrayed strong feeling, respect, and love for the tragic gentleman who sat palely in the great chair and eyed me like I was ten thousand miles away.

And then I remembered Mr. Treet's advice concerning questions, ignorance, and the art of being a gentleman. I held my tongue and smiled. Which, if nothing else, had the effect of terminating the interview . . .

albeit with a sigh. I left the room with a powerful resolve that on the morrow I'd be more forthcoming and respond better to my father's moods. Other resolves I had, too, among which was a firm one to see my uncle hanged, shot, or otherwise rewarded for the damage he'd wrought in our lives.

I went in search of Joseph. Found him all too easily. Begged to see the portrait again. Cheerfully, Joseph obliged. I studied it—Joseph at my elbow. Burned the face into my mind. Marked each slippery feature . . . took comfort for the weak chin. Took fright from the subtle smile!

"A real murderous gentleman, that," murmured Joseph. "Every now and then a Dexter turns out so. Black as night, Mr. George, sir."

I tried to imagine what thirteen years might have done to the face—and to the soul. No cheerful result was got. I began to see him in odd corners . . . or as a shadow, passing a window or crossing the lawn.

There was a bolt on the inside of my bedroom door. I slid it to—and the rusty iron screamed like a sinner in Hell. To my relief, no one noticed, no one heard. . . .

Next day my father seemed more of his old self—as if the strong news of yesterday had suffered a dilution by his generally amiable spirits. He ventured a few paces across the room, leaning heavily on my arm and making much of it. I was sensible of the privilege of supporting him—even without my mother's ironical looks. Dr. Newby opined that by the end of the week he might venture as far as the great hall . . . and come to no great harm. But under no circumstances was he to venture into the air. I think Dr. Newby knew of my uncle's escape and dreaded he might be lurking in the park, awaiting a second, more prosperous chance. Did my mother know of it? Most likely, yes, for several times I saw her stare out of the windows sharply . . . with an expression at once angry and alarmed. And she opposed, almost violently, Sir John's intention of going out into the drive one frostily sunny morning in curt defiance of his physician.

But he was a man not easily deflected, having, under his ordinary gentleness of manner, a powerful will and a great strength of character that seemed to overcome even physical weakness.

"Madam," he said, "this boy will support me—even if you will not."

So we went out onto the terrace and, very unequally, down to the drive, anxiously watched through the windows, for my mother refused to countenance the excursion by joining it.

Despite efforts to the contrary, he leaned on me very heavily, and was forced to stop every few paces to regain breath.

"You and I!" he kept murmuring—then smiling in an almost bitter fashion . . . as if ashamed of his wretched condition.

To distract him, I pointed to the silver birch copse that began less than a hundred yards away and extended almost to the village. Here, the perpetual mists still clung and clotted in the fine-drawn foliage, so that it was impossible to judge of the copse's undergrowth and denseness. I suspected it to be a good place for game. It seemed I was mistook. Vastly.

The copse was a place where some pursued item of Royalty had once taken refuge and there rewarded an earlier Dexter for some particular service. One did not trample and hunt like a vulgar farmer in such a spot. One preserved such a spot together with one's good name. One was not an animal. One was a Dexter. Even if one had been brought up in low company one should have respect. . . .

Life with the Treets had taught me—among other things—to bear with humiliation (even the most painful) without much show of distress. I studied the copse. Fancied something glinted in it. Distracted myself with imagining what it might be.

"Boy," said my father, quietly. "I did not mean to hurt you. But . . . but I'm glad that I did. For I saw you did me the honor of being gentlemanly. I saw you struggle not to betray yourself . . . not to betray yourself into reproaching me for the pain that I'd caused. I—I could not wish for more from my son than that."

Thoughts of leaving the Manor at once departed. I began to understand my father. A difficult, prickly, austere man, but, like certain roughly cased fruits, marvelously rich within.

Once again, something glinted in the copse—metallically. I said, uneasily, "Shall we go in now, sir? You must be tired. . . ."

Afterwards, Joseph murmured to me, "You saw? You saw, Mr. George, sir?"

"Saw what?"

"In the copse. He's there. Armed. Lurking. The Captain!"

· 8 ·

JOSEPH WAS wrong. Happily so. He'd seen a lurking and a glinting in the copse—and forthwith leaped to his unpleasant conclusion. True, he'd looked before he'd leaped, but any man may do that and still end up in the ditch. Nonetheless, till it was known who'd been in the copse, he wore a terrific air of conspiracy as discreetly as a new hat. His eyes, which never so much burned as spluttered (for they were mostly moist), hunted me out everywhere and seemed to urge me into the wood. ("Mr. George, sir—it's your duty . . . Mr. George, sir—even as you was once his victim, now he must be yours! This house's nature demands it! Death to the Captain—at your hand!")

Another footman being abed with the ague—the mists having got to his bones—it fell to Joseph to oil and polish the weapons in the gun room. He understood I was partial to pistols and muskets. So was he. Noble objects, wasn't they! Even Christian.

"Christian?" I asked.

"Indeed, Mr. George, sir. For they render the weak equal to the strong. Thus, a lad, not full grown—save in name and honor—may, with a fine-chased pistol, prevail over the greatest villain in the world!"

"And be hanged for it?"

"What? Not in self-defense, Mr. George, sir! Where's your law?"

"Self-defense? Then the great villain has a pistol too? And maybe is a better shot? And then won't be hanged on account of self-defense?"

"Oh! Mr. George, sir!" exclaimed Joseph, reproachfully. "You're as cunning as a stage full of monkeys!" He came down heavily on "stage," as if to insinuate that my low-class upbringing was clouding my judgment. "And, was I a betting man, I'd wager all on a lad like you! Vastly quick, vastly witty, and afraid of naught! Courage, Mr. George, sir! That's your strength!"

He went on like this awhile longer, subtly urging me to come to the gun room with him. For he plainly hoped I'd choose a weapon and go out and shoot the Captain dead.

But not just for the joy of a bang, a scream, and a thud, for Joseph, in spite of his secondhand bloodthirstiness, loved my father entirely, and longed to see him avenged. Also, he was fond of me—on account of my parentage—and conceived me to be incomplete while my murderous uncle lived and so sapped my honor as a Dexter.

What he suggested and urged and pricked me on to was for the good of the House—and no skin off his nose, one way or the other. . . .

So it came almost as a blow to him when it was discovered that the lurker in the copse had not been the malevolent Captain. Which, on considering it, would have been a vastly rash place for that queer, mysterious, and evil man to've fled to. His portrait had suggested a gent of some subtlety and deviousness—a gent of some consideration for his own security no less than for his brother's ruin. . . . God knew where he'd gone to from Newgate! But one thing was sure: he'd not escaped merely to parade himself in front of the outraged eyes of Joseph!

I breathed a sigh of relief. Not that I'm anything of a coward, but, being a genius—like the Treets—I've an amazing imagination that permits me to see, in my mind's eye, a whole course of events plunging to horrible disaster! And in such close and particular detail (smells, screams, and agony all to the very life!) that sometimes I'll sit, transfixed with horror, in the midst of calmness with no more to set me on than a humble bumblebee buzzing somewhere aloft!

The lurker in the copse had been (thank God! thank God!) Mrs. Montague! And the glinting had been the sunlight on her jet necklace and silver crucifix, which she always wore as if to show she was an accredited agent to both spirit worlds—the light and the dark.

She came out of the copse just before half-past three o'clock, and struggled unequally up the drive, as if in much doubt as to the wisdom and propriety of her course. Which doubt, we afterward learned, had caused her to lurk in the copse for several hours, growing colder and rheumier by the minute, while she'd debated with herself (and, maybe, with her spirits too) whether or not to call at the house.

At times it had seemed like tempting Providence, for no charges had been brought against her by Sir John or Lady Dexter. And charges might well have been brought, for witchcraft . . . to say nothing of false pretenses.

"And then, ma'am," went on that sour-faced lady, taking tea in my mother's parlor, "the memory of our thirteen amiable years overcame me, and, come what may, I resolved to face out your and Sir John's displeasure in order to beg your pardons and forgiveness!"

My mother nodded coldly, and offered her an oat cake, which she took like it was the Sacrament.

She bit into it and began to snivel and dab at her bright, black-button eyes as if nervous they was coming loose. Such little things—the delicacies of the house, the pattern on the china, and the old, tapestried chair on which she'd always sat—had dwelt in her memory mournfully in these past weeks. Her tears were of pleasure . . . like she was spirited back to the home of her childhood, with all its joys as fresh as they were in her heart. . . .

"Not that my home had anything of such grandeur and dignity about it, dear Lady Dexter," she added apologetically. "But it was a place I loved, ma'am."

My mother shrugged her shoulders and said she'd never had any intention of depriving Mrs. Montague of the happiness of visiting, and, indeed, would be ever content to receive her, though, of course, with certain differences. . . . Here, she turned her head and looked at me inscrutably. (My father was not present, being tired from his morning's walk, and, in any event, an infrequent visitor to my mother's parlor.)

A heavy silence came over the two ladies, and first my mother, and then Mrs. Montague, stared at a three-legged, country-style table that stood in a corner of the room. It was at this table, I learned, that they'd always sat when communicating with the dead infant who'd claimed to be me.

"Ma'am," said Mrs. Montague, solemnly, "I swear to you I was more deceived than deceiving!"

"Indeed, I hope so!" remarked my mother, coolly. "For if Sir John or I had thought otherwise, you'd be in a vastly less agreeable place than where you now sit, Mrs. Montague!"

Mrs. Montague blinked hard at the little table, as if there was some obscure deception in its very wood.

"Lied to by a dead child!" she muttered. "What is there left to trust in?"

"Why! The living, Mrs. Montague!" exclaimed my mother.

"Yes, indeed, ma'am! And I'm glad that I should have been proved a foolish, mistook old woman by so handsome and lively a young man! My downfall has been your wonderful gain, Lady Dexter! And how much nobler he is than the complaining babe who deceived to take his place! Oh! Wicked, wicked ghost!"

I wondered whether I ought to defend the discredited spirit—or merely smile genteelly and hold my tongue. Mrs. Montague, her white hands on her black lap, was regarding me with all the openness she was capable of while my mother fidgeted irritably with the tea things, as if to say, "Well, George, say something!"

I said, "How soon it grows dark at this time of the year. The evenings are drawing in—"

"A hint!" cried Mrs. Montague, nervously. "I do believe, ma'am, that Master George has given me a hint that I've stayed too long!"

"George," said my mother, her face somewhat flushed. "I take it that you merely spoke out of a foolish desire to say something—and consequently meant nothing. I take it that you did not intend to be ungentlemanly. So I'll not ask you to apologize—for you'd have to beg pardon for being either a fool or a lout! Mrs. Montague—pray accept *my* apologies! And take another cup of tea, ma'am! I'll not hear of your leaving till five o'clock!"

By the time she'd done the moment was past for explaining I'd only intended to change the course of what had become an awkward conversation. So I was left with a most unjust depression and a shrewd desire to change places with the infant I'd dispossessed.

"George! Mrs. Montague has been asking about Mr. Treet!"

My mother's voice brought me back with a start. "Mr. Treet. Your foster father. Have you forgot him so soon? Come, sir! You may talk about him!"

This was truly extraordinary. All past efforts I'd made to mention the Treets had been frowned upon. So all I could presume was that Mrs. Montague was sufficiently low class not to be offended.

"A genius," I said. "A vastly great man. A tremendous brain. Really wonderful."

From the corner of my eye I saw my mother, midway between a sneer and a smile, but she held her peace and let me go on. Which I did, warmly and at length . . . more to impress *her* than to gratify Mrs. Montague's curiosity.

I listed Mr. Treet's accomplishments and triumphs: his dignity, his standing in the profession, his elegance and wit, his gentility and kindness, his learning and depth, and, in general, the stupendously grand character of that remarkable and much-undervalued man. To which latter end I touched briefly on his misfortunes, for I felt that some explanation was required for such a prodigy's lack of much success.

Mrs. Montague nodded. "He sounds a very good sort of man."

"Good God!" exclaimed my mother. "A genius, no

less! Even with a half of what we've been told! I hope he was not offended by being given a thousand pound! For I understand your geniuses are very apt to fly off the handle if they feel themselves to be slighted or patronized!"

I did not see her face, but I suspected it to be as ironical as ever. I said, as coolly as I was able:

"I'm sure he took it as what he'd have expected from Sir John and Lady Dexter—a courtesy, Mother."

I didn't feel it necessary to mention Mr. Treet's absolute jubilation over his windfall, for that was private . . . between him and me.

My mother said, "Good heavens, Mrs. Montague! It's close upon five o'clock! 'Tis when you wished to leave! Oh forgive me, ma'am, for keeping you gossiping when you must have been longing to be on your way! And after you'd *said* five o'clock."

Mrs. Montague looked somewhat taken aback—then rose to go as if "five o'clock" had been *her* idea in the first place. I almost thought so myself, for my mother was the adeptest person I'd ever known at such genteel arts as speeding the non-parting guest.

And it was then, in some odd fashion, I found myself quite close to Mrs. Montague. She still wore her look of foolish confusion—so I was entirely unprepared for what happened next.

"Be in the copse at six!" she breathed, and, as she did so, her eyes momentarily sharpened, as if they were indeed poor black buttons, abruptly tightened on their threads.

My mother, I was certain, had heard nothing.

She declined a carriage, or even a servant to accompany her, and I watched her cross the terrace and begin to descend the steps onto the drive. There was already a quantity of darkness in the air, and she seemed to mix with it at the edges, so to speak. Then she appeared to hesitate . . . and a sudden patch of white, blooming in her person, betrayed she'd turned her head to stare back at the house. Then she set off again, with a queer, rocking motion, as if she was being stirred . . . there being something in her substance that was dissolvable in the night.

For many minutes after she'd disappeared I stared into the shifting darkness, fancying her outline still visible . . . sometimes on the drive, sometimes on the grass, and sometimes walking sturdily some yards in the air above the ground.

I wondered how long she'd wait in the copse before giving me up, for I felt no obligation to keep the appointment. For what could she want with me? What secrets could there be that dared not be breathed in the house? Indeed, what secrets at all?

Could she, perhaps, be planning to confront me with the lying ghost of the dead infant and so force it to scream "Pardon!" of the fat lady in black who'd tempted it from the grave?

Came ten minutes to six o'clock (amazingly quick!) and still I could find no more reason in Mrs. Montague's whispered demand.

Unless she needed money? And was uneasy about asking my mother direct? (Understandably, all things considered!) Who, then, could she ask, but me? No one. So now she was in the damp, dark mists of the copse, counting on the kindness and courtesy of the young gentleman. Doubtless, she intended to beg me to intercede with my mother on her behalf. The thought appealed. ("Mother, your friend is in need!" And spoke with a fine, reproachful air. Hmm!)

I left the house at five minutes to six o'clock, convinced I'd hit on the right solution. Which conviction stayed with me across the terrace and for some thirty yards of the drive. Then, when I turned onto the wet, soft grass and made toward the dark bulk of the copse, that conviction began to waver— even to fade.

Of a sudden it seemed remarkably unlikely that the sinister Mrs. Montague was in such straits as only I could save her.

A new thought tackled my brain like a humorous spider. Being, so to speak, in the trade of ghosts, was it not possible that portly Mrs. Montague designed to add me to her stock? And ease me onto her grim shelf by slipping a bodkin into my heart?

The air was thick and much cumbered with the salty smell of the sea mists, which never left the copse or its vicinity.

"God rest ye merry, gentlemen . . ."

I began to sing in a clear, strong voice, for it was the season of carols and good cheer.

"Let nothing you dismay . . ."

The copse was close grown . . . much tangled . . . appallingly dark, and infected with a plague of rustlings and whisperings and abrupt silences.

"Remember Christ, our Savior,
Was born on Christmas Day!"

My voice had took on an odd, secret quality as if, sing as loud as I might, it would never be heard beyond the wood.

"To save poor souls from Satan's power
Which long have gone astray."

The gaunt silver birches, much clogged with pale bundles of mist, seemed somehow to be moving as I passed them by . . . indifferently . . . as if they was busy bleached skeletons—inhabitants of a dead city—going about grave business, in pairs and threes . . . crossing streets, gossiping soundlessly on corners. . . .

"And it's tidings of comfort and joy!"

She was not come! It was past six o'clock and neither stitch nor stain of her! I was arrived in a clearing, dimly silvered by a finger of moonlight. As sure as anything, the place for a meeting! No Mrs. Montague.

"Comfort and joy! Comfort and joy!"

The tarnished trunks of the birches stood off from the clearing, and seemed to shape the darknesses between them, till the eye, confused by dull light and profound dark, saw it all in queer reversal . . . thus the black between the trees seemed the substance, and the light, the illusion. Of a sudden, I fancied I was stood amid fifty or more enormous coffins, between whose edges gleamed a bleached and bony light.

"Comfort and . . ."

Something moved! In one of the coffins. A shape. Dark. Tall. Moving with a limp. Not Mrs. Montague. But a man. He came slowly, formidably, out of his coffin. In dark regimentals . . . much torn . . . like a half-pay officer in Death's army. And, even before I saw his face, I knew him. It was the Captain. I had been trapped!

· 9 ·

I CONSIDERED my last hour not only come but on the point of being gone. I considered Mrs. Montague to be the most monstrous soul this side of Hell, and with a fair claim to the same distinction on the other side it. For it was she who'd obliged the Devil in the person of my Uncle Dexter. Which devil now squatted on a tree stump and stared at me with eyes as dark, deep, and round as pistol muzzles. One of his stockings was torn and bloody about the ankle, most likely from the wrenching off of a leg iron. The injury looked some days old, and was beginning to smell it. He blinked and shifted his foot from under my nervous scrutiny.

"Not very elegant for an officer, eh?"

I shook my head—and wondered if his pistol was primed.

"How is my brother?" he asked abruptly, and gave the same curious smile that the painter had caught in his portrait.

"My father is recovering—"

"Your father? Oh yes . . . yes . . . I'm your uncle,

ain't I! Hmm! Uncle Richard? Uncle Dick? No. Just call me Uncle Dexter. Till we're better acquainted."

. He was smiling down at his pistol—which he'd laid across his lap as he talked—and I conceived that his expression was as much a disability as a reflection of his mind. Also I conceived that, could I but gain the edge of the clearing before he shot me, I'd be able to outpace him, by reason of his stinking wound.

"Nephew George," he said, almost grinning now, and still at his damned pistol, which, I saw with interest, was not cocked. "You ain't—um—you ain't got twenty guineas about you? Ha! Soldiers is always on short commons! The penalty of serving! Payment in honor! And would ye believe our Colonel's name is Rich! Tight-fisted as Broughton!

"Or ten guineas, nephew—if twenty enfilades you? Debts, y'know. Landlord of the Dog. Pressing. Old mother Montague. Real bloodsucker. Can't let the family down, my boy, can we! Ah! Can see by your face that ten's a volley of musketry in your pocket! What about five? Or e'en one? Ha—ha! I'll be honest with you, nephew! Five shillings'd be as welcome as a porker in a siege! Till the end o' the month, of course!"

I considered that I was dreaming, or, rather, that I'd been dreaming till now. For this grinning, scowling, somewhat shifty gentleman in his ragged regimentals (red coat almost black with filth and sweat, and buttons leaving little epitaphs of thread all down his facings to mark where they'd fallen) was extraordinarily real. The monstrous Captain Richard Dexter! Short of five shillings! (Till the end of the month, of course!)

He peered up at me with his nervous smile.

"Well, nephew?"

Thirteen years had not done much damage to his face, beyond sinking his eyes somewhat, and folding up the skin beneath them like an ill-made bed.

"For d'you see," he went on, "I left every last six-pence with your Aunt Dexter and your cousins—their need being nearly tremendous."

Helplessly, I fished about my person and produced, not five, but seven shillings.

"You're a gentleman, nephew! A real gentleman! Ha—ha! Saved my life, you have!"

He took the seven shillings and stowed them away in his waistcoat, which he patted affectionately, and remarked:

"Reserves to the rescue! Sergeant Shilling and six recruits!"

He grinned and scratched at his ankle with his pistol barrel, declaring that itching boded healing. He seemed entirely at his ease, of which state he had, at that time, an absolute monopoly . . . there being, in that damp, dark, and sinister place, barely sufficient for one.

To say that my only thought at that time was of escape is to do me an injustice. I had some three or four other thoughts as well, but they never seemed to amount to much. So I apologized for having no more money than I'd given him—and offered to go back directly for more.

He stared up at me in some astonishment, and for the first time there was no smile on his face . . . which looked, in the close, oppressive dark where he sat, like some mottled moon flower, patched, stained, and un-wholesome. I suspected he was on the point of shooting me and I estimated I might fling myself sideways as his finger tightened on the trigger . . . but not before, else he'd change his aim. (Always provided I was not rooted in terror and a rapt contemplation of my past life passing before me on account of my last moment having come.)

"I ain't a beggar, y'know, boy!"

Good God! I'd offended him! A new fashion in villains! Nothing behind-the-times about this Dexter. No out-of-date snarlishness nor old-world broody hate! But a sensitive villain—with some show of amiability, even— save when offended. . . . And why not? Would the Devil himself be any less disquieting if he was, say, shabby as a lawyer's clerk, with a crooked smile and an itching palm; apologizing, even, as poor souls crashed and screamed through his shoddy pockets to the everlasting night of fire?

"D'you think," he went on, his voice growing high-pitched with his odd passion, "that I bolted from damned Newgate and ran and limped, and crawled and dragged through stinking ditches and down roads that was worse for six horrible days—in mortal terror of everything that moved—for to beg seven shillings off something between a child and a man?"

(There seemed to be no advantage in reminding him he'd begun by asking for twenty guineas.)

"D'you think me so abject that I've forgot my wife and children left in despair—and feel nothing of being the outcast of the world? D'you think I come to my childhood home (My God! My God!) more wretched than a whipped footpad (ten times more wretched— for he's lived in the filth, not fallen into it and like to drown!)—come to my home, I say, by night and creep about in this old, dark, fearful place—plagued with wet aches and a burning foot all for the sake of alms from my mighty nephew?"

His voice, shrill as knives, seemed to've cut a bundle

of mist, loosely tied in the invisible high branches, so's it came undone and drifted down in solemn loops and nooses . . . like the ghost of a hangman's rope fumbling for its proper home about my uncle's neck.

His passion seemed to've subsided. He shivered and grinned . . . begged pardon, saying that much privation might unhinge even an officer and gentleman. He was not ordinarily so wild, but of an equable disposition. On which score I might ask my Aunt Dexter. He prodded at his military-style wig (much disturbed by his adventures) with his pistol barrel and pushed it back so's his reddish hair appeared like an injury at the limit of his moon-wet brow.

So why had he come to haunt the dark copse, with crooked smile and straight pistol? (Which pistol was a very handsome affair . . . a gentleman's weapon, being mounted with silver, indistinctly engraved.) I believe I'd have asked him—if something else hadn't intervened. A cracking of twigs, and then a rustling.

"What was that?"

"A cat. An owl. Maybe even a fox, Uncle Dexter—"

"Too heavy!"

"The night's deceiving, and the air's still—"

"Or is it you that's deceiving?"

He was no longer sitting, but crouching, rather—and his eyes were swollen with alarm.

"Deceiving?"

"You laid information! Betrayed me!"

"I never knew you was here!"

He let go of my wrist, which he'd seized, and I straightened the small, plainish lace Lady Dexter had thought sufficient for my years and country situation.

There was silence in the wood, save for the noise of breathing. The damp had got to my seedy uncle's chest.

It bubbled sullenly on each extremity of drawn breath. The tall, skinny trees stood at the edges of the clearing like the limits of the natural world . . . beyond which lay the turbulent quiet of the grave, where worms roared into bony eyes and weeds snapped ribs with the racket of musket fire. . . .

Again the sound of cracking! And closer at hand—

"Then you was followed!"

"I left quietly. Not seen—"

He snatched at my sleeve and dragged me down beside him. Then he recollected his pistol, presented it to my head, and offered to ventilate the same should I utter a word. The grass was thick and cold and wet— and had a curious, sweetish smell, not unlike stewed ale. (Or was it my uncle's breath? For it beat in my face like a fist.)

The cracking and rustling grew louder, and there came a soft thump of feet. Whose? Joseph's? Or the constables', who'd somehow picked up the Captain's trail?

"You foul little treacherous Dexter!" breathed my uncle. " 'Tis the damned constables! But you'll not live to sneer and inherit!"

I believe I owe my life to that curious, confused, devilish man's lack of application as a soldier (and to Colonel Rich's tolerating of it!), for he'd still failed to cock his pistol so's his finger stumbled on the trigger. And then his tide ebbed and mine was risen—for the third person in the wood came blundering into the clearing, crying:

"Mr. Richard! Master George! I pray to God you ain't killed each other! Mr. Richard! Master George! I pray to God you ain't joined the ghosts."

It was sick-faced Mrs. Montague—much torn, plucked

at, and diminished by her passage between low branches and high bushes! Mrs. Montague, shaking like a fat black jelly with the cold and with alarm for what her go-betweenishness might have done!

"Madam!" cried my uncle, leaping up from concealment so that, to this minute, I still see half his face caught in the moonlight and grinning like all its flesh had been stripped away. "Madam! No harm's done! This dear boy and me is now acquainted! Come, nephew! It's Mrs. Montague!"

"Thank the Lord!" gasped Mrs. Montague, her button eyes fastening first on the pistol, then on my eternity face. "I'd a sudden fear that—it came upon me before I reached home—I conceived that— Oh! 'Tis the penalty for being a seer!"

Now was the time for me to depart, for I doubted if he'd shoot after me in sight of a witness—however partial. And I would have gone—was on the point of it—when Mrs. Montague, ruefully regarding the rips and rents in her black gown, said:

"Have you asked him, Mr. Richard?"

"Why no, ma'am. We'd scarce met when we heard you and—ha! ha!—took you for the Law!"

"Then you must ask him now! After all, Mr. Richard— he's your kin. And flesh and blood, you know. . . ."

"Flesh and blood!" said my uncle, coolly. "We all know the qualities peculiar to those commodities, ma'am. Corruption and degeneration. Give me men of stone! They, at least, change not—"

"Nor do they bleed!"

"Nephew! You speak without thinking! You know nothing of the affair! Nothing you—"

"Mr. Richard!" warned Mrs. Montague, standing beside my uncle and somewhat behind him so's she looked like his profound shadow and darker soul. "First ask. Then dispute."

Ask what? What had she and he brewed up between them for my drinking in?

"A reconciliation, nephew. That's what I'm here for. No more, no less. 'Tis my only chance in the world. And it ain't for myself alone. (Myself? Soldiers learn to endure. To stand alone . . . save for the company of the dark gent with the white face and hands. I mean Death, nephew!) Your Aunt Dexter . . . your three cousins. Theirs is the misery that drives me. And to what citadel? A reconciliation with your father. Through you, nephew. Be my ambassador. For his great joy on your return must render him susceptible to your persuading. Tell him, boy—tell him in your own time and in your own way that I never meant him to be hit. Dear God! He seemed to *fall* into the path of my shot! For I swear to Heaven it was an accident! He turned and tripped. Slipped sideways and caught my charge in the gut. Had he but stayed upright, no blood would have been shed— save, maybe, mine! Tell him that! For pity's sake, tell him!"

"Indeed you must tell him, Master George," murmured Mrs. Montague, clasping and unclasping her hands.

My uncle was grinning and scowling in the most extraordinary fashion. Suddenly, I thought he was mad. A vastly comforting notion in the circumstances—what with the dark wood, the veiled moonlight, and sinister, ghost-raising Mrs. Montague, planted beside the hungry madman like a black toadstool. My spirits, which, before the notion of my uncle's madness, had risen, suffered now a sensible decline.

I said I would do what I could, and hoped I sounded amiable and obliging. Mrs. Montague nodded—but my uncle grew impatient.

"Tomorrow, eh, nephew? You'll mention it tomorrow?"

"Give me more time than that, Uncle Dexter. My father has scarce got over his wound . . . let alone that *other* injury—"

"Other injury? What d'you mean, boy?"

"Why—the abduction, sir. Your abducting me when—"

"Oh my God! My God!" He shifted, glanced for the tree stump, and sank upon it, while his head dropped into his waiting hands as if without them it would have continued down to the grass. And from this security, being muffled and hidden, his voice protested the most extraordinary thing! He was innocent! Absolutely! Entirely! Neither he nor his agents—(Agents? Ha—ha! What money had *he* to spare for third parties when the first party was so penurious! Did I know what a soldier was paid—*if* he was paid? Agents? Ha!)—neither he nor his agents had had any part in the sinister affair of thirteen years before.

He raised his head momentarily from its concealment and displayed an expression of ironical honesty. From Mrs. Montague he'd learned the details of my upbringing. Did I think he'd sixty guineas a year to spare from Dexters more hungry, more needy—and vastly more close?

He paused, and made some efforts to straighten his wig, which was all but off and uncovering limp tufts of his hair standing out of his pate like stuffing. . . . He never knew, he said, who'd first implicated him, but he'd come to believe it must have been the Principal in the affair—the dark abductor himself.

And when he, my loving uncle, had heard of my

return, most naturally he'd thought the secret villain was revealed—and honest Captain Dexter absolved. His heart had soared; his hopes had risen; and his ship had stood fair in the wind.

But it seemed he was mistook. (Here, he popped his head once more into his hands to signify despair and dismay.) He was finished; done; destroyed. For if I could not help him—who could?

"God," interposed Mrs. Montague. "And His ministers beyond the grave."

A most terrific silence seemed suddenly enjoined on the three of us following this, and Mrs. Montague cocked an ear. . . . I hoped she wasn't taking instruction from the dead infant who'd deceived her before, for it wasn't hard to imagine a piping little voice crying in the dripping branches:

"It ain't Captain Richard! It ain't Captain Richard!"—all for the sake of a passing rescue from the wet and windy tomb and a warm dry place in Mrs. M.'s heart.

("God rest you, bony gentleman—
Let nothing you disturb!")

From far off came the sound of a clock striking. Uneasily, I said I'd be missed if I stayed longer. My uncle looked undecided, glanced to Mrs. Montague—who nodded, as if to say, " 'Tis all right, Mr. Richard. Let him go now. We've shook his heart and poisoned his brain. He's partly ours and will return. All will go our way, Mr. Richard. Let him go."

"Till tomorrow, nephew! Till tomorrow!" called my uncle—and I turned to look back at them. Their faces were no longer clear, but, as they stood side by side, there was something in their shared attitude that betrayed a shared smile.

During the night the image of the uncanny pair kept

appearing before my closed eyes, and their mutual smile grew as broad, deep, and crooked as the Devil's Dyke.

For if my lame and armed uncle was not the Principal—who was? In God's name, who could it be—if Mrs. Montague and her constabulary of the dead should prove him innocent?

· 10 ·

DECEMBER SEVENTEEN—and, though the weather was dullish, misty, and inclined to a thin, floating rain, there was a remarkable fine burst of sunshine in the small front parlor to the left of the hall. At half-past ten o'clock Mr. Treet called! Indeed! Mr. Thomas Treet! The great man himself—full of smiles and proud genius. He'd paid his respects to my father and congratulated him on his recovery (which was fast becoming complete—though he still tired easily and slept much).

"And now for you, George! My respects and congratulations! Gentlemanly! Yes, indeed! Lap of luxury! Security. Golden future. Love all round! Couldn't wish for more!"

He seemed so cheered to see me that I made no mention of such trifles as a murderous uncle, a cold, curt mother, and a general air of graveyard politics that flavored the air like a rancid sauce.

For Mr. Treet seemed to have troubles of his own. Not that he paraded them. Indeed, to an outside eye, as he paced the window wall like he was measuring it for improvement, he was the very image of a prosperous talent at evens with the world . . . so's it would have seemed an impertinence to remark on his bandaged hand, the plaster on his forehead, and the injury to the top of his wig, which still smelled strong of singeing.

I asked after the remaining Treets.

"Well. All well, George."

"Are they in London, Mr. Treet, sir?"

"London?" He spoke with bitterness, unusual for such a man. "That sooty seat of pig ignorance and matchwood? No, George. They are in Shoreham, awaiting a ship. Fresh worlds to conquer, my boy! The horizon beckons!"

I hoped his ship would be in better trim than my heart, which sank abruptly under his news. But I said nothing of that and only asked him how had London failed and so gone down in his esteem. (For London had always figured high in his ambitions and been a happy contrast to the pig ignorance of Sandwich, Deal, Faversham, and Rye.)

He stopped his pacing and sat down in the window seat, resting his hands on his tightly shining knees.

"A triumph, George. We had a great triumph." His fine face, which had been momentarily overcast, began to glow in its old fashion and his eyes shone proudly. "In the Duke's Theater in the Haymarket. The middle of the world, George. We performed *Saul and the Witch at Endor*."

"With the 'Devil's Fire,' sir?"

"The 'Devil's Fire'—'Lucifer's Smoke'—everything, George!"

He was smiling now, and blinking rapidly as his eyes grew moist at the memory.

"The 'Lucifer's Smoke' at Sandwich was but a wisp compared with this! Dark! Rich! Passionate!"

"Berlin Syrup, Mr. Treet, sir?"

"A whole pint of it, George!"

"I'd like to've been there!"

"Indeed—you should have been! Hotspur! Jane! Edward! All of us—I tell you, George—was I not a man of science, I'd swear the spirits of the old philosophers was in the billows with us, whispering and singing all the secrets of the invisible world! And then—and then the 'Devil's Fire'! The grandest ever! Dwarfing the smoke like it never was!"

He was up on his feet again, pacing the window with his hands clasped behind his back.

"And yet, sir . . . ?" I said sadly, for tragedy lurked in his bearing, giving him a most melancholy dignity.

"Where there's pig ignorance, George, the grandest triumph is forgot and blotted out by a single speck of disaster. But—but no matter! I didn't call to burden you! Think of us at our flood tide, my dear! Think of us at one with the mysteries of Nature! Think of us as the tremendous Treets—and ask no more. And if you have seventy pound for our passage to Virginia, we'll be grateful but not humble. And if you've not, we'll love you just the same, dear George!"

"Then the thousand pound . . . ?"

"Gone," said Mr. Treet, soberly, then waved his large hand and bade me not think of it. "Think instead of the 'Devil's Fire,' George, with . . . with . . ."

"With Crystals of Lemon, sir?" I murmured, not supposing he'd used that powerful substance. "Not Crystals of Lemon?"

"Yes, indeed." Mr. Treet smiled grandly. "Crystals of Lemon, George. Four ounces. (For was we not in the middle of the world?) And the grandeur of it! The spectacle! The fiery glory such as kings might gape at!"

"But the danger, sir . . ."

"All grand and adventurous things bear their meed of danger, George. 'Tis the spice of beauty and the sauce of joy!"

"And—and then what, sir?"

"The theater burned down," said Mr. Treet, simply, and sat down. "The curtain went up like it had been soaked in gin; then the whole, poor pack of matchwood crackled and roared to total extinction."

He frowned at the memory and touched the patch of plaster on his forehead. Mercifully, no lives had been lost and such injuries (he raised his bandaged hand) as he'd suffered had been the fault of the manager. He, Mr. Treet, had had to go back into the terrible inferno to drag forth that whimpering conniving man who still held the note for a thousand pound against damage and rent.

"Madman!" the despicable creature had screamed, rolling in the streaming street to douse his smoldering clothes. " 'Setting off a blaze like Mount Vesuvius'—he was an Italian, George, vastly excitable—'on a wooden stage! I'll have you in the Castello'—he meant the Tower, George—'for this!' "

" 'Sir,' I said, guiding him out of the way of the chain of water buckets all London seemed to've turned out for, 'you have my note for a thousand pound—' 'Foolish, crazy man! *Five* thousand ain't enough for the damage you've done!'

"There was no advantage in arguing with him. He was—as the saying goes—beside himself—and a vastly unattractive pair he made! So we left, George—forth-

with, straightway, and together—me and the Treets
mounted our conveyance and shook the dust—or, rather,
the mud, for the inhabitants of the Haymarket had
been prodigal with water!—of London from our feet!"

He sighed and frilled his bandage like it was the
finest Holland lace.

"One speck of disaster and all triumphs is forgot!
Dark, glowing billows . . . fiery caves . . . cauldrons
tremendous with supernatural passions . . . all nothing!
Hmm! Nothing. But not to you and us, George! *We*
know what to remember. So don't be burdened, dear
boy. Forget what I've said—and, if you can visit, we
are all at the Old Ship Inn at Shoreham. With or
without the seventy pound, George, you will be vastly
welcome! God bless you, my dear!"

On which amiable note, we parted—Mr. Treet to his
horse and a bumpy waving down the drive till he disappeared where it skirted the copse, and me to a profound study of how best I could come by the seventy
pound that stood between my good friends and greatness over the sea.

Mr. Treet's visit came, as I've said, like a burst of
sunshine on a gray day, and continued to shine for
some while after he'd gone . . . there being so little of
the sinister, eerie, or uncanny about him. Not that he
was one of the lace-bosomed gentry whom you may
look clean through to the other side. There was much
to Mr. Treet, but it was all of an agreeable brightness,
and such spirits as *he* conjured up had never had the
misfortune to be dead. While his lack of seventy pound
seemed a properer part of him than his one-time posses-
sion of a thousand!

I did not think there was anything disquieting about

his mentioning it, nor disturbing about his visit itself—
until I'd kept my appointment with my shabby uncle in
the copse. That my father was angered by Mr. Treet's
appearing I heard only from Joseph, who had conspiracy-
shaped ears and often heard what had never took place,
for my father had said nothing to me. While my mother,
on the other hand, had been unusually affable and
trusted that my visitor had not been offended by her
not taking sherry with him. I said, "No," and she smiled.

This must have been after five o'clock, for I was
considering applying to her for the seventy pound Mr.
Treet stood in need of, but decided against it as six
o'clock stood ominously near.

He was there, of course, before me—and complaining of the penetrating wet. He had, I noticed, changed
his stockings, but otherwise looked no better than on
the night before. I gave him a piece of game pie and a
bottle of brandy I'd brought under my coat. He looked
surprised, then took them with a "Provisions for a
regiment!"—and added he hoped the regiment wasn't
to follow, for he was uneasy that I'd broke my word and
betrayed him.

"I never gave my word, Uncle Dexter!"

"Beg pardon, nephew! But I thought we'd met under
a flag of truce!"

I asked him where he was living, but he shook his
head and grinned.

"I'll not tempt you, nephew. For you might talk in
your sleep. Just leave me and my bivouac as the secret
of the copse. Until our business is done, eh? And may it
be soon—for this mist and hellish damp will be the
death of me!"

Then Mrs. Montague, carrying a lantern, joined us,

and the queerest council of war began. The army: an
uneasy heir, a fugitive Captain, and a fat old lady dressed
in black (with, maybe, as many inquisitive specters as
might prove uncoffinable). The Enemy? The Principal
(for my uncle still swore his innocence with a passion).
Our weapon? Memory (and, maybe, Mrs. Montague's
friends).

First, my uncle talked of the Stranger . . . the
thirty-guinea man. Had the Stranger ever, in an unguarded moment, let slip a name—or even a piece of
one?

He never had an unguarded moment. A very discreet
sentry of his tongue.

What did he look like?

Drought-faced—by which I meant his skin was all
cracked like the earth in want of rain. I believed him to
be a deep snuff-taker, for the folds about his nose
seemed much clogged with it. His eyes I supposed to
be of a waterish blue, but could not take my oath on it
for I never saw him in daylight.

My uncle looked puzzled, even perplexed, then shook
his head.

"Further back," murmured Mrs. Montague. "We must
look further back."

She stared into the twitching lantern flame, which
cast changing shadows across her face, seeming to alter
her expression without her knowledge of it. I suspected
her of inquiring of her friends, the dead.

"And we find something strange," she said at length.
"A certain Mr. Treet."

(Mr. Treet? What had *he* done—save be a gentle
genius? His name sounded out of place in the present
company.)

Mrs. Montague continued, "For odd Mr. Treet told

that the infant was brought to him during a certain thunderstorm in June."

"So?" said my uncle. "I remember that June. Vastly well."

"Then d'you remember, Mr. Richard, that, on the day the child vanished from the Manor, there *was* no storm? Indeed, the weather was cruelly splendid. There was no thunderstorm for a full week. Surely you recall? The heartbreaking searches—day and night? D'you recall being incommoded by the weather? No. And yet Mr. Treet described—a storm . . . when there was none. Strange . . ."

As when I'd first heard of these dark affairs at the beginning of my life, cold shadows seemed to pass across my heart.

"That's true, ma'am," said my uncle, staring thoughtfully into the moving shadows thrown by the lantern light . . . so's the copse seemed now like a double image, for wherever there was mist, the shadows of the trees stood black and firm in the air, ten times more real and profound than their papery, silver-gray counterparts—from which the black trees seemed to've been unwrapped. "That's true. I remember very well. I remember the house being filled with guests—for it was George's birthday." He turned to me. "A great occasion—for it was thought very miraculous that you'd come to it and still alive. You was a weakly child, nephew, and none of your brothers had made six months, so your first birthday was in the way of a victory."

"And then," chimed in Mrs. Montague, "the evening when it was discovered you was gone. Horrible. Lady Dexter, white as a shroud—Mrs. Smith, your drunken nurse, in fits and tears! God knew who was going to tell your father . . . for he was visiting somewhere. Then, when he came in—saw the pallor and dismay where he'd left flushes and good cheer—he half guessed. Horrible . . . horrible . . ."

"And then when gypsies were blamed," put in my uncle.

"Till it was recalled there was none in the neighborhood," remembered Mrs. Montague, "save the player, Mr. Treet, of course. Odd man . . . even strange . . ."

They went on awhile longer—each taking up on the heels of the other as they recalled that distracted time . . . as if, somewhere, somehow, a deeper truth would be found, lying neglected and forgot in a dark corner.

"But who gained from the child's abduction?" said Mrs. Montague, suddenly. "Save you, Mr. Richard?"

"I swear I'm innocent!" cried my uncle, staring at Mrs. Montague as if she'd turned on him.

" 'Tis the entail that's the stumbling block. For none but you, your dear wife and children gain upon that account."

"They, too? They, too?" exclaimed my uncle, tragically. "Is none of us clear, then? The damned entail!"

"Ten times damned!" agreed Mrs. Montague. "Ain't it, Master George—to plague an innocent family so?"

Helplessly, I nodded. They was crouched on either side of me—unwholesomely close—so that to turn from one meant confronting the other. There was no escape.

"So let's overlook the entail," whispered Mrs. Montague—as though the entail was a high, cruel mountain that nothing heavier than a whisper could clear. "Consider what other gaining there could be. Who else profited?"

(Here, my heart began to beat quickly, and the night seemed colder than ever before.)

"No one," said my uncle somberly.

"Not even—not even *Mr. Treet*? What of the thousand pound he was given? And above all, what of the deep hold—thirteen years deep—he's gained over his foster child? Ain't there profit there, Mr. Richard? Think of Mr. Treet, who was *mistook* about the storm. Mr. Treet, who *happened* to be on hand. An interesting person, that! What if—what if he and the nurse, Mrs. Smith, had an agreement? Ain't things clearer so?"

They'd begun to nod together, that unholy pair—and desperately I searched for a contradiction to stop them.

"What of the Stranger and his thirty guineas twice a year? Where did Mrs. Smith find so much? And why send it to Mr. Treet?"

"Did you *count* the thirty guineas? Or was you *told* of it? Ah! You was told! And, I fancy, merely to mystify you. I think the Stranger was, maybe, *Mr.* Smith, come to see if all was well, with—as like as not—a few shillings toward your upkeep as a gesture of—of ill faith."

"No! No! I don't believe it! There *must* be someone else!"

"Who, Master George? Tell me who—and I'll oblige and believe."

And my uncle echoed, "Who, nephew? Tell us who—and we'll oblige and believe." And he continued nodding in time with Mrs. Montague till I felt that nothing less than the stoppage of their dark hearts would put an end to it.

"Maybe Mr. Craddock knows something of Mr. Treet," said my uncle.

"Mr. Craddock?"

"My brother's lawyer. Close as an owl. But Craddock knows everything. Write to Craddock, nephew—at Lincoln's Inn Fields. Yes, indeed, Craddock knows everything."

"Save what's beyond the grave," said Mrs. Montague, smiling disagreeably.

My uncle shrugged his shoulders and Mrs. Montague, still smiling, delivered—though she could never have guessed it—her deepest, deadliest thrust of all.

"Master George, love and honor Mr. Treet if you will. He may yet prove innocent. But—if he's guilty and has gained your affection for profit—mark well my words—soon he'll call upon you and ask for money. Beware, Master George. Beware of this—for it will be the beginning of his ends!"

· 11 ·

SO MR. Treet stood accused. By whom? A fat old bag with button eyes who'd taken instruction for thirteen years from a dead little gentleman who'd lied himself out of the ground. And? A seedy ruffian who'd all but murdered his brother, been jailed for it, escaped . . . and now lurked, armed, near his brother's house. A vastly reliable pair!

So why was I awake, then, halfway through the night, sweating and much perturbed? An obscure problem gnawed, mouse-like, at my mind—a trifling problem, a tiny-toothed nothing, compared with the huge structure it had set itself to destroy, viz, my faith in Mr. Treet. (But a mouse may eat away a mountain—if it's made of cheese!)

He, Mr. Treet, had told me he'd guessed where I'd come from, on that disputed night long ago. Then why had he not returned me for thirteen years? Why? Why? Why?

No! It was impossible to suspect him of being the Principal. The act was too dingily vile . . . too black.

For it *was* black. Not on account of depriving an infant of his home and heritage—but on account of the ruin it had wrought in that infant's home, and the hatred it had engendered between two brothers. Hatred to the point of murder. The blasting of my father's life and joy, the curdling of my mother's heart . . . and, not least, the changing of my uncle (should Mr. Treet prove guilty and he, innocent) from Richard Dexter, gentleman, into a seedy ruffian of no account.

But why had Mr. Treet waited for thirteen years? Some good reason . . . some excellent, good reason . . . And the strange mistake about the storm? . . . The mouse was breeding—the mountain trembled. God forbid it should turn out to be cheese!

I determined to write to Mr. Craddock—not for my uncle's sake, nor even for Mr. Treet's, but for my father's sake—and my own. I judged that the landlord of the Shepherd and Dog would dispatch the letter for me, and hold his tongue on account of being flattered by my asking him. I'd written the letter and was intending to visit him midmorning, to which end I was very gently dressed. A piece of good fortune, that, for, before I could leave, there were visitors. Remarkable visitors—even amazing!

As usual, Joseph brought the news. Somewhat out of breath. His smooth face was flushed with excitement . . . by which I took the news to be distracting, for he never looked half so pleased as when he'd a touch of calamity to bring. He'd knocked and come in directly, observed my letter still on the escritoire, but was too full of information to take it in.

"Mr. George, sir—they've come!"

Who'd come? My Aunt Dexter and her three sons,

John, Edmund, and Bertram! Arrived in an equipage that, if it had ever seen better days, had long since forgot them. Likewise, their clothing. Wouldn't be surprised if Mrs. Dexter was genteelly entertaining bugs. A real smell of Newgate about them all!

It seemed they'd all expected to meet with the Captain. Indeed, they'd come with high hopes of the family rift having been healed. ("On account of the restoration of your dear self, Mr. George, sir. Is it possible your terrible uncle deceived them too?")

My mother—much shaken and nervously angry—had begged them say nothing of the escape to Sir John, for his heart was still in some danger. Whereupon, Mrs. D. ("Your aunt, alas, Mr. George, sir.") had gone as white as her complexion allowed, for she was of a florid countenance, besides being much stained from travel. Did she understand that things was no better than ever they'd been? Even was they worse? Her dear boys! Her dear boys! They'd come, not out of the lion's mouth, but down into his boiling belly!

"In a word, Mr. George, sir—they have cast themselves upon our mercy. And, in a word, they will have fallen upon thorns."

All this was delivered in a rapid murmur, for Joseph always kept his voice low, as if afraid it would be shot at if raised up. Also he was shifting from foot to foot in some agitation, for Sir John had been told of the arrival—and Joseph was desperate not to miss a word of the Newgate Dexters' reception. He urged me to hurry; then, not waiting, made off himself in a discreet haste.

They were still in the great hall—the Newgate branch of the family—forming not so much a group as a bundle. My cousins . . . two of them tall, thin, and dark-haired, the third, somewhat shorter and plumper with the only cheerful face among them. I suspected him of being something of an oddment, for his cheerfulness seemed to derive more from his mother's and brothers' discomfiture than from any inward peace.

"I beg of you," my mother was saying with some urgency, "leave now! Go to the village—or even to Shoreham. I'll send money. I'll help you! But, I implore you, madam—go now! Before *he* sees you!"

"My brother-in-law, ma'am! I've—we've come all this way! I would *like* to see him! Flesh and blood, ma'am! Flesh and blood!"

My aunt, a large-bosomed lady with some remains of handsomeness, was equally urgent, and her voice was loud and clear—having been much burnished by years of ill usage.

"It will do you no good, madam! Nothing will come of it but aggravation and distress!"

"Flesh and blood, ma'am, flesh and blood!" repeated my aunt, twitching at her stained green gown, while her youngest son seemed vastly entertained, as if his mother's remark was too worn a favorite to be taken with aught but a sly grin.

At which point I was about to join them, for, being so absolutely taken up with her own concerns—my aunt in making herself heard throughout the house and my mother striving, by her pale agitation, to prevent it—they'd not yet seen me standing by.

But my father came first. He brushed by, bringing a faint smell of the ointment Dr. Newby always larded on his bandage. I never heard him approach, being, I suppose, absorbed in the family reunion. I do not think he'd overheard more of my aunt's bawling than her last two "flesh and bloods," for his expression and complexion were equable—even amiable.

My aunt stopped in mid-sentence—likewise my cousins stiffened in pleased respect. My aunt, seeing my father's gentle looks, began to smile—and shot my mother an interesting look. Then my father halted, leaned heavily on his stick, and said to my mother:

"Madam. We must be hospitable. Take these unfortunate people and see they are rested and fed. Doubtless, they've traveled far, and have still farther to go."

He said nothing more. Not a single word to my aunt and cousins—scarce even a look. Then he turned and went slowly back toward his room, ignoring Joseph's offer of assistance (for that person had appeared beside him, so full of solicitude that it fairly ran over and onto the floor) with a shake of his head.

My mother looked somewhat taken aback, but my aunt, remarkably enough, looked quite satisfied with her reception . . . and seemed to've missed entirely that, though my father had indeed greeted them as flesh and blood, the manner of it had been more suited to a horse than to his nephews and sister-in-law. She preened herself and remarked:

"My brother-in-law looks well, don't he, ma'am! And, you see, it did no harm to wait on him! He looked quite cheered to see us! Flesh and blood will tell, ma'am!"

But my cousins did not look so satisfied. The older ones seemed very sensible of the rebuff—and even the youngest's grin had turned ferocious.

My mother was drawing them away, and there was much shedding of cloaks and coats—like a dingy autumn—when I thought I might fairly be introduced. But again I was prevented, this time by Joseph, who crept up beside me and murmured:

"In the library, Mr. George, sir; Sir John wishes you to go to him directly."

He was standing by the window, looking out. (I wondered if he'd seen anything in the copse, but thought it unlikely as the mists were heavy that morning, there being much moisture in the air.) He did not turn at once so's I'd time to notice a change in the room. A trifling change, inasmuch as it was the substitution of something for nothing. The empty frame that had once held my uncle's portrait was now filled by a Dexter of the last century, a stone-faced gentleman whose undoubted red hair was hid under a full-bottomed wig. A great-grandfather? Vaguely I wondered if, in years to come, I'd take my place beside him, be similarly varnished into a sour mood, and be stared at by another young Dexter who'd wonder why his relatives rarely smiled. And another Joseph would murmur:

"Your great-uncle George. Grim, ain't he!"

Then my father spoke, still without turning.

"The—the unfortunate people who've come to us . . . I'd have you be amiable to them, boy. Your—the sons are not to be blamed. I'd have you treat them with some respect, not deal with them as—as servants or beggars. Though beggars they are and must be! Their mother is a foolish and stupid person. Maybe she's more to blame than one supposes? But, nonetheless, she, too, is unfortunate. The victim of an unequal marriage—unequal in birth, understanding, and ambition."

Abruptly, he faced me—and I saw his excellent face was somber and tragic . . . as if much more lay behind it than his words expressed, so that I wondered if there was some queerer and darker secret yet than even Joseph dreamed of.

"You have the advantage, now, boy. Clothes, home, servants, and—and name. While *they* have nothing but the name. Nothing but that! And you—you are well-grown, well-featured, even well-liked! Almost too much, eh?" His lips spread in a smile, but his eyes remained deeply unhappy. "I charge you, boy, if you hope for my friendship and—and love, take no more advantages than those you have. I would have you be gentle with our visitors."

His eyes flickered round the walls to where, between the tall Newgates of books (for all the shelves were strictly barred), hung Dexters to the time of Queen Mary, cool gentlemen whose smiles were as rare as the philosophers' stone, gentlemen whom death had not so much claimed, as come to, cowl in hand, with a "By your leave, sir—but would you condescend to come this way?" And then, maybe, they'd smiled. . . .

At last, my father's eyes met mine—and I strove to return his look with all the pallid dignity that was hanging on the walls. His expression softened . . . grew almost tender; then he bade me go and join the visitors.

"But remember, boy. Remember my wishes."

They were in my mother's parlor—that small, rich, elegant, dainty room with its chairs and side tables so delicate and spindle-shanked that it seemed a discourtesy to eat in their presence, the only sturdy item being the country-style round table at which Mrs. Montague's dead little gentleman had paid his deceitful respects.

"George," said my mother. "Here is your aunt and cousins."

My aunt made a great show of turning in her seat and

staring at me with wide-opened eyes, as if I was more remarkable than I'd supposed.

"I fancy he takes more after your family, ma'am," she said at length, "for he don't look much like my brother-in-law. Excepting in color of hair, that is." (My mother's hair was dark, save where it was touched with gray.)

"But he's a good, healthful look about him, which is wonderful when one considers what an ailing babe he was! 'Tis the country air, ma'am! My boys would have benefited, I fancy. Yes, indeed . . . but then they're taller grown. Even my youngest. By a full inch! Stand up, Bertram, so's your aunt and me can see how much taller you are than cousin George."

But he would not. He scowled and sat awkwardly, protesting a headache. I thought he might be ashamed of his ill-fitting breeches and coat (being too plainly descended from one of his brothers), and so felt sorry for him. But afterward I discovered his general disobligingness was due to nothing more amazing than a disagreeable nature.

"A headache, my love?" cried his mother; then to Lady Dexter: "I fear he may have taken a chill, ma'am! For, though he's tall, he's delicate. Such a tragedy for a child! It prevents so much. So often, ma'am, when he should be happy in company, he's afflicted! 'Tis the overelegance of his nature, I fancy! A real Dexter, ain't he!"

Satisfied that he'd caused some commotion, my cousin began to grin again, and only remembered to scowl whenever his mother inquired after his health.

We stayed in my mother's parlor for about half an hour, during which time I discovered my two remaining cousins to be pleasant, though lacking in genius, and even my aunt to have some admirable qualities, viz, a cheerful wit and a way of relating adventures entertainingly. It was, I found, no hardship to obey my father's wishes with regard to *them*, and there were some very genteel exchanges between us. I fancy I made an agreeable impression on everyone present. Except on my cousin Bertram. And on him, I considered, nothing—absolutely nothing!—would have made a more satisfying impression than a fist or a boot.

But my father's wishes were strong in my mind, and I returned his scowls and sneers with as pleasant looks as I was able . . . once, even, asking him myself if his head still ached. This was when a servant had come to tell my mother that a meal was served and there was, consequently, a general movement toward the door. He stared at me sullenly, then muttered:

"I hate you, Cousin George! I wish you was dead!"

· 12 ·

MY LETTER to Mr. Craddock was gone! I'd
forgot it entirely in the excitement of the new arrivals,
and not remembered it till the following morning. And
then Joseph came to my room and explained he'd taken
the liberty of sealing and dispatching it during the
previous day. Uneasily, I thanked him. He smiled . . .
and remained standing by the door, for he never seemed
to commit himself to the middle of a room. Then he
murmured, as if as an afterthought:

"And, begging your pardon, Mr. George, sir, as you'd
not writ the name very clear, I took the further liberty
of glancing within so's I might direct the letter without
troubling you. . . ." Here, he paused . . . maybe to see
if I was disturbed. I said nothing, and he nodded—
more with his eyes than his head. "I think, Mr. George,
sir, you have been deceived . . . most likely by Mrs.
Montague."

He watched the effect of his words carefully, till he
was satisfied he'd hit on the truth. It *had* been that
mysterious lady who'd urged me to write to Mr.

Craddock for information about Mr. Treet and whether or not *he* could have been the Principal.

For, said Joseph, now thoroughly at ease and staring at the escritoire as if to see if anything else had been written that might have escaped him, Mrs. Montague was and always had been a particular friend to Captain Richard. Had she told me that? And had she told me that she'd been an acquaintance of my aunt before the marriage and, maybe, had pushed that unlucky affair forward? And had she told me that the drunken, neglectful Mrs. Smith—that nurse who'd once let me fall on the terrace and then capped her career with sleeping whilst I was stolen—had she told me that that same wretched Mrs. Smith had been *her* recommendation?

"No, Mr. George, sir—such evidence as I conceive she's given you against Mr. Treet is nothing compared with the plain guilt of Captain Richard and her own most likely complicity! Mark my words, Mr. George, sir—if you'll pardon the liberty—your abduction, and all its tragic consequences, depended on the entail, and on nothing else. The entail—a terrible, beautiful, grand, and horrible thing. Yet vastly noble, Mr. George, sir."

With that, he went with his finger to his lips, and smiling somewhat—as if he'd suddenly sensed a conversation elsewhere in the house that he was particularly anxious not to miss.

When he was gone, for one reason or another, I began to feel quite cheerful. Not that I'd any particular cause—for my life still seemed to be clogged with uneasiness and mystery—but into my mind's eye had trundled a large wagon drawn by a wise old horse. "Otway," I murmured, and smiled.

I began to whistle, and strolled to the oak linen chest. After a moment I opened it and looked down on

my glorious coat and waistcoat, my red-heeled shoes
. . . and a fine wig I'd not even worn. So the Treets
were in Shoreham! Warmly, I longed to see them—to
dispute with Edward, to be genteel with Jane and
financial with Rose, even to wake Hotspur and hear
him howl! And proud Mr. Treet himself . . . at whom
much mud had been thrown—but none had stuck! I
took out the wig and tried it on. "Magnificent!" I exclaimed, involuntarily.

Came a knock on the door. Thinking it was Joseph I
said grandly, "Enter!"

It was my mother. My mood froze. Her eyes fixed on
my wig—then went to the opened chest. To my amazement I saw they were suddenly rich with tears! Hastily,
I took off the wig, believing I'd caused her pain. She
said:

"You looked splendid in it, George! Indeed, you
did!"

Then, as if not trusting herself to say any more, she
left me.

I never discovered why she came—nor why she departed so soon. But she left behind her an odd sense of
warmth that made me wish, with all my heart, that she
was more mistress over her own capriciousness, for her
good moods were as handsome as anyone's in the world.
But they lasted for so short a while . . . too short, alas,
for my daring to ask her for seventy pound. For my
thoughts were still strongly with Mr. Treet and his
great need.

I judged that my father's temper was steadier—and
less liable to sudden change. I stared thoughtfully out
of the window. . . .

It was a crisp and handsome day, much gilded with
winter sunshine, and with the never-departing mists in

the copse drawn up close about the trees—like thick wool petticoats about a host of silver ankles. . . .

Yet somewhere within it was my evil uncle. Had he seen his wife and sons arrive? Was he, even, signaling to them? Or had they already met? I doubted that. My aunt could never have held her tongue.

Even now I could hear her, loudly overtalking the housekeeper, for she and my cousins were on a tour of the house. They'd been invited to stay till after Christmas, which I took as an omen of my father's pliant mood. Would that mood bend further I wondered? Would it bend as far as seventy pound?

Dr. Newby had come and gone. A brief visit, which meant my father's health was steady. For the doctor had no conversation outside of his trade, and felt ill at ease with the well, fidgeting off as soon as he could. Being a small man, and vain, he found he could stand high only when his companion was lying down.

It was close upon ten o'clock, and I supposed my father to be in the library. Which was a real satisfaction. For, of late, it had become his favorite room, being quiet, calm, and peaceful. . . . In that room he always seemed most at peace with himself and the world. The shadows that so often seemed to cloud his eyes and darken his brow were there dispersed, and his strong, admirable face was seen to have a gentleness most encouraging. (In my mind's eye I saw his smile of assent as I mentioned the seventy pound. "Seventy pound? Certainly, boy. You shall have it. And wish Mr. Treet a calm sea and a prosperous voyage.")

It was in the library, surrounded as we were by Dexters past, and the world's wisdom, that we seemed most close together—and of a like mind, spirit, and heart. Here he'd talked—and still did—of excursions he and I would take (Dr. Newby permitting), riding side by side through the landscape—even into the night. "What of footpads, sir?" I'd sensibly asked, for, when I'd been a Treet, darkness had been no friend. "Why, boy!" he'd laughed. "With your skill in arms, I'll look to you to guard me from all trouble, sorrow, and hurt!"

And lately—but yesterday it had been, after he'd recovered from the amazement of the arrivals—he'd quite warmed to the subject of Christmas to come, and the dozen or so neighbors he hoped would honor us with their presence. This last matter caused him to smile a good deal and say that he hoped I'd distinguish myself in dancing with the ladies, but not too much, for I should remember they were simple country folk, not very courtly in the ballroom nor nimble upon the floor. Indeed, I was cheerful at the thought of the library, and even hummed as I went:

"God rest me merry gentleman,
Let nothing me dismay!"

He was not there. Instead, sprawled indolently upon the window seat was my cousin Bertram. A very disagreeable discovery. Even disheartening. Maybe, had my mood not begun so high, its dropping off might not have seemed so plain.

"I was looking for my father," I began.

My cousin made no reply, but continued to sprawl and stare sullenly. He looked ill—or sickly, rather.

"Is your head troubling you, Cousin Bertram?"

"Not half so much as you, George Dexter."

"I'm sorry for that—"

"Why? Did you fancy we'd be friends?"

"No. Nor enemies, neither. It's all on your side." I remembered my father's wish . . . and refused to be drawn further. I shrugged my shoulders and began to walk away.

"D'you know, Cousin George, you walk like a common, showy player? And wear your clothes like one? And talk like one? Which ain't surprising, for my mother says you was brought up by vagabonds. Why didn't you stay with them, *Cousin* George? For no matter what blood runs in your veins, it wets a vagabond's heart!"

"Talking of blood, Cousin Bertram—your nose is bleeding."

He raised his hand, touched at his nose, then examined the result.

"You're mistook, Vagabond George."

"No, no! And your eye—the right one—is black and swollen. And more . . . your cheeks are patched and much bruised! Your hair is half pulled out! Your ears are near dragged off! Your—"

"W-what d'you mean?"

"Oh forgive me, Cousin Bertram! It's a terrible gift I learned from my vagabonds. The gift of second sight. Sometimes I see things just before they come to pass! Dear Cousin Bertram—I hope to God I was mistook, but you looked for the moment like you was beaten half to death!"

I'd frightened him. A not very remarkable accomplishment—considering his somewhat dingy spirit. He was crouching back in the seat with his hand raised against . . . God knew what! The air? A tired fly? Then, slowly, he dropped his hand and resumed his sprawl.

"A dirty, spiteful player's trick! I think you are sly, vain, coarse, and hateful! I think you are full of scorn and contempt and self-importance! I think you fancy yourself better than us because you're cleverer! Cleverness is slyness, George Vagabond—and what passed

for quality in the playhouse and in the street turns out
to be as coarse as old rope in a family like ours! Ask my
uncle! Ask my aunt! Ask them what they *really* think of
you! Even ask my mother—who thinks you too smart
by half! They're all ashamed of you, George Vagabond—
and every step you take and every word you speak puts
a curl to their lips and a prick in their hearts!"

His unpleasant pale face was blotched and swollen
with spite, while his small blue eyes—deep-set, like
they'd been pushed too far into overlarge sockets—had
begun to puddle with tears. I never saw a youth so
venomously angry nor so full of extraordinary hate.

"You're mad!" I said. "You ought to be in Bedlam!"

He began to jeer. "Oh yes, George Vagabond! All the
world's mad save you!"

"You're vicious, stupid, and—"

"And not so clever as you, George Vagabond?"

"No! And not so clever as the dirtiest candle snuffer
who ever earned his keep for an honest night's work!
You dingy little beggar who's never earned a farthing
save by holding out his hand and whining, 'I was born
to a gentleman, sir! Please support me!' What use are
you in the world, Bertram Dexter, but to stop your
brothers' clothes from rotting in a closet? You scare-
crow! I'd have fought with you—if I'd thought you was
worth it! But I'll not touch you—so there's no need to
squint and cringe! For, though your name is Dexter,
you'll never be a man if you live another hundred years!
You're rubbish, Bertram Dexter. A sickly parcel of
rubbish—no matter what coat of arms was on your
wrapping!"

I believe I went on awhile longer in a like vein, but
richer, as more and more comparisons between disgust-
ing objects and my sprawling, sullen, blotched cousin

came to me. Thirteen years of life with the Treets had given me much to draw upon . . . and a tongue to give it substance.

"And if I'm showy, cousin, it's because I'm worth showing . . . while you—you are like a dingy property, fit for nothing but to keep the wind out of the privy! An inn privy, cousin—that's what you bring to mind!"

I stopped—to draw breath—and I heard the most terrible sound in the world. A sigh, as bitter as death. My father was in the room. Had been standing in the doorway. Listening. Observed by Bertram—who'd held his peace as close as a poisoned dagger.

"Father . . ."

The doorway was dark behind him. He stood as if in a great, somber frame. His face was white as bone—and gave a formidable depth to his eyes . . . which seemed to've sunk so far that the light in them was all but extinguished. . . .

"Father . . ."

Abruptly, he turned—and departed. Without another look—or a single word. Then my cousin stood up and walked past me with an unpleasant smile.

"You were right, George Vagabond. There's some things it's best not to show!"

When he, too, had gone, I looked uneasily about the walls at the Dexters who remained—the dead and varnished Dexters of long ago. Grimly, even scornfully, they stared down—all save one, who seemed to be smiling. A youthful, splendid Dexter, in a brown, full-bottomed wig and steel breastplate. He was turned half toward me, and pointing, with a curious smile. Pointing at what? A bloody battlefield. Of a sudden his smile seemed more alarming than all the somber scowls, for he was smiling at agony, blood, and death. And it was the self-same smile I'd seen upon my shabby uncle—the lurker in the copse.

I went to the window and stared mournfully in the general direction of Shoreham and the Treets. Though the sun still shone, the day no longer seemed so prosperous an occasion for asking my father for seventy pound.

For the rest of that unpleasant day I wavered between seeking out my father and asking his pardon for my outburst—and going off to Shoreham and leaving the house forever. More and more, as the day wore on (or, rather, wore out, for it grew ragged and threadbare and incapable of keeping out the cold) I leaned toward Shoreham. My father was plainly avoiding me. If ever I saw him, crossing a passage, or entering a room, a somber urgency seemed to've driven him elsewhere when I arrived. And, even as he avoided, so my cousin appeared—leaning against a wall, sprawled in a chair, loitering in the hall . . . sometimes grinning, sometimes murmuring as I passed him:

"I'll destroy you, George Vagabond. Yes, indeed, I will!"

I thought, briefly, of applying to my mother, for she seemed more amiable than usual, but she was much taken up with listening to Mrs. Dexter. Also, memories of her ordinary coolness and ironical air made me hesitate to ask for anything which, being refused, would injure me—both in her eyes and my own.

And so to dinner, in a gloomy mood that was made abruptly worse. My father had decided to break his habit of eating alone. He was sat in the great chair at the head of the table. Somberly, I regarded the six silver salt cellars, and reflected that five would have sufficed. *My* meal was like to be bitter enough without unnecessary addition. I took my place and found myself opposing John, my eldest cousin, who was took so much by surprise by grace that it was very nearly "For what I've already swallowed, may the Lord make me truly thankful!"

And then my father looked at me—and smiled! This was extraordinary! Had he forgot?

"Well, boy—are you and my nephew friends at last? For surely, after this morning's storm, there should be a sunny calm! After what I overheard, there cannot be a dram of anger left in you! All came out in a tempest! Madam!" He addressed my mother. "This morning, in the library! Such oratory! Rich and fiery! I was amazed!"

"Indeed?" said my mother, coolly.

"Indeed, indeed, madam! And I'll tell you, was he not fourteen, and our nephew fifteen, the mortality of his expressions and the passion of his tongue would have come to a duel! Oh madam, madam! I promise you, at first—and for some hours afterward—I was angry and even afraid! For it seemed as if all our house would come tumbling about our ears under this fierce new spirit that had entered it! But then, as the day endured—so did I! No sounds of war. Instead of drums, the beating of young hearts. And now I see them both at table. All eyes bright, none swollen. So can we be angry, madam, when they are not?"

I sat and listened to him in amazement. And then grew ashamed of being amazed that my own father was warm, compassionate, and understanding. I began to entertain some doubts of my own powers of judgment. I looked up and down the table . . . and up and down my life. I wondered what other mistakes I might have made. I began to feel very humble and pleasant and peaceful. Then, by degrees, warm and full of confidence. . . .

Between the syllabub and cheese I leaned over and asked my father for seventy pound. He toyed with his wineglass. Stared into it. Looked up along the table to my mother, then briefly to me.

"Why, boy? Why seventy pound?"

I told him. Again, he paused—for somewhat longer than I cared. There was an odd air of measurement and weighing in that pause. Then he said:

"Tomorrow, boy, take a horse and ride to Shoreham. And take also, not seventy, but a hundred pound for your Mr. Treet. Seventy for his passage and thirty for—for whatever you will!"

As the saying goes, I could scarce believe my ears, and, from that moment on, till I was in bed and on the point of sleep, I suspected them of lying to me for no purpose but to cause mischief, dismay, and disaster. My own ears!

· 13 ·

"HERE IS the hundred pound, Mr. George, sir—and here, as they say, is your father's blessing for a safe journey and a quick return."

Thus Joseph, as he handed me a leather purse and a pistol with silver chasing.

"Between here and Shoreham, there's a real autumn of cutpurses, footpads, and vagrants. Ha—ha! Not so much thick as thieves, Mr. George, sir—but thick as leaves!"

He waved off the stable boy who'd brought my horse— then murmured confidentially, "But it's not such poor objects that need alarm you so much as—*you know who*! God forbid that you should meet him, but if He's overruled by the Devil, and a certain Captain should stand in your path . . . well, Mr. George, sir, there's a charge in this barrel you may confidently levy upon him—and so let daylight into his abominable dark head!"

I thanked him, and wondered if he suspected that the Captain and me were already acquainted. I did not think so, for Mrs. Montague had been the only witness to our meetings, and she, quiet soul, kept as close counsel as her friends underground.

God was overruled by the Devil at about half a mile from the house, where the drive yielded to the road, and skirted the copse.

"Halt! Stop! Nephew!"

My uncle—seeming to've fallen out of the trees like an old, blackened stump. For in daylight he looked more ragged and wretched than ever.

"Is it—is it true they're up at the house? My sweet quartermaster and my darling colors? In a word, nephew, my wife and sons?"

I'd reined in, and he limped up beside me and laid a hold on the bridle. My hand went to my pistol—and my thoughts to my purse!

"For God's sake, child! Would you shoot your own flesh and blood?"

Before I could tell him—out of the wood came Mrs. Montague. A vastly early bird, very partial to the worms.

How, in Heaven's name, had she known I was to be out and about? My uncle was for being mysterious, but the lady snapped him off as quick as a toad.

"There's enough mystery, shadows, and darkness in his origins, Mr. Richard, without murking him the more. 'Tis nothing extraordinary, Master George. 'Tis nothing more wonderful than that leaky vessel, Joseph, visiting the Shepherd and Dog last night in company with my servant."

My uncle shrugged his shoulders and grinned.

"The lady's right, nephew. Better to lay such cards as we have on the table. For we're all on the same side, ain't we? No sense in hiding trifles from each other." He patted my horse's neck, and went on, "So you've met my dear arms and ammunition! Tell me, nephew, ain't they splendid? Your aunt—my wife—handsome! Of course she suffers from not being at her best! But you should see her when she's money and fine clothes! A duchess, nephew! A general's lady! 'Tis but harsh deprivation that's brought her low! And her sons! True, John ain't overshrewd—indeed, he's fit for naught but to inherit. But then—so's the Prince of Wales! He's a gent, nephew—and I love him. I hear you fell out with Bertram. Ah, well—I admit, Bertram's an oddment. But there's some good in him! But dig deep enough and look hard enough, and you'll find it. Indeed, you will! Bound to! Ah! My troops—my sweet troops! How I long to see 'em!"

I felt a sudden pity for this ruined soldier who loved his family in spite of themselves. Then Mrs. Montague said:

"So Mr. Treet is to receive an early harvest, Master George? A hundred pound."

"A harvest? What do you mean, ma'am?"

"No more than I say, and have said before. The first touch of the leech is light. But once fastened, he'll suck and suck and suck till you're dry and bloodless as a bone."

"You're mistook, ma'am. It's money for passage overseas. I'll not see him more—"

"Let's hope you're right, Master George. Let's hope your affection ain't betrayed. Let's hope he's what you think he is . . . and not what I fear he might be!"

My uncle was staring at the ground.

"A hundred pound, nephew? A real bone-crusher of a purseload, there! And all for Mr. Treet? Could you not—um—outflank a little platoon of guineas this way? Flesh and blood, y'know. . . ."

I thought carefully. All too plain, he'd nothing immediate to hope for, save money. For he couldn't subsist in vagabondage much longer. So if I gave him the extra thirty pound, there was some sort of a chance that he'd seize on it as a bolt-hole to better things. (Such as a ship to the Indies?)

"Thirty pound, nephew! You're a prince! There, Mrs. Montague, ain't he a prince? I asked for a platoon—and he gives a whole regiment! Flesh and blood, ma'am! There's nothing like it!"

Then there happened something I'll not quickly forget. My uncle, having stowed away his capital, was staring at my pistol, which was in the saddle holster.

"Show me, child! Come! I'm a military man. Arms is my occupation. Let me see it!"

I hesitated.

"Child—child! I'll not keep it!"

I pulled the weapon out—and showed it to him. He stared at it; took it in both hands; examined it shrewdly.

"Who gave it to you?"

"Joseph."

"He knows naught of arms! Did anyone study it first?"

"I—I don't know."

He took out his own pistol, which was the twin of mine.

"Here, child—take this. For if you'd fired your own, it would have, most likely, blown your head off! The barrel's cracked. Very neatly. Almost as if it had been done a-purpose. D'you see? There—above the chasing. I'd swear they were chisel marks! Once saw it done in the regiment. Barrel dented in so's the ball caught and the charge blew backward into a poor devil's face! Hmm!

Lucky you halted, child. Else you might have halted farther on—more permanently."

I galloped on to Shoreham in a desperate mixture of moods. My joy at being bound for the Treets was much tempered by a strong panic! If my uncle had spoke the truth (and he'd exchanged pistols too quick for me to be sure), then someone was set on emptying the world of me!

My thoughts went directly to Bertram! His words, which I'd took at the time as but a piece of natural peevishness, stood now as meaningful. "I'll destroy you, George Vagabond!"

Bertram Dexter! The soldier's son! Most likely knowledgeable about weapons; most likely had heard the tragic tale of the regiment. (Most likely had enjoyed it too!)

"You deadly young gentleman!" I muttered—and shivered in my saddle. For in all my born days I'd known nothing stronger than an egg or a turnip flung from the pit when I'd performed ill—or an envious push or pinch when I was performing too well. But never a threat to my life itself! Save, of course, at my life's beginning—at the hand of the Principal. . . .

Then I grew calmer, and achieved a sort of smile as I thought on the horrible shock to Bertram when I returned whole and alive!

I arrived in Shoreham at half after eleven o'clock. The Ship Inn. A pleasant, low-built, snug, appetizing place upon the harbor side of the main street . . . and much distinguished by a ship's figurehead fastened above the door, which figurehead bore, I discovered, a striking resemblance to the landlord, who had the same bland, varnished look as the wooden sailor . . . and no more sense, either.

He, the landlord, was stood bolt upright in the dim parlor, looking for all the world like he'd just been took down from outside by the bailiffs to be sold up. (He oiled himself, Hotspur Treet assured me excitedly, and whiffed like an old fish.)

But first, how the Treets appeared. It was most marvelous. The parlor was quiet—inhabited, it seemed, by the landlord alone. Then there was a creaking, and a scraping, and an scuffling, and an obscure whispering— and they came!

Out of quiet nooks! Out of empty chairs! From under impossible tables (where there was no room for a mouse, let alone Henry, Nell, and Hotspur!), and even from behind the unmoving landlord himself!

The Treets! The parlor was full of them! And the uproar! Imagine how "It's George! He's come!" can have sounded, shouted, shrieked, and fairly roared by six strong voices, separately and together, for a full minute without pause! Never had there been a reception like it—though it had been but a month since we'd parted!

I tried to defend myself—for I was instantly swarmed on—even shouted out to Miss Treet (dear Jane):

"I thought you was going to be more polite this time!"

But nothing was heard for my voice was too like theirs, and mixed in like a pint of wine in the roaring sea!

"How genteel he's dressed!"

"How dull!"

"Such fine lace! Costly!"

"But very—very *quiet*!"

"Like a mouse?"

"Ah! but a rich mouse!"

"A *cathedral* mouth? George ith a cathedral mouth! Ha-ha!"

"Be quiet, Hotspur! He's not had a chance to talk! Give him air! Let's hear his news!"

So they gave me air. Sat me down and—before I could open my mouth—began to tell me *their* news! The London adventure! All the grandeur, the splendor, the glory . . . the fire and water, till my head began to fizz and crackle like the old timber itself! I'd forgot what it was like to be talked at by six geniuses at once!

To be heard at all one had to shout and bang the table . . . even, maybe, to pull an ear or two.

"*Lend* me your ears!" I roared—like I did in the old days—and they all laughed and gave way.

But I'd only *begun* on my adventures when historical Edward asked, "But what have you found out, George? Have you discovered the Principal? For it seems to me—and I've given it much thought—that it's very important you should know."

I looked at him, suddenly longing to confide—when he made, by chance, a chilling remark.

"For I'd have thought, George, considering all past family histories, that villains don't give up on first attempt. What with your return—well, he must be brooding on other ways. For, if you was unwelcome when you was one, you're bound to be fourteen times as unwelcome now! To someone!"

"Edward!" said Miss Treet sharply. "That's a sour and miserable thing to say! For George is welcome everywhere!"

Edward looked surprised. "It wasn't meant to be miserable. It was interesting. I wish I was in George's shoes with a grand mystery like his! Indeed I do!"

And so do I! I thought, from the bottom of my heart,

for I'd remembered the pistol, and was wondering, for the first time, whether it had *really* been Bertram, or was there someone else . . . ?

Then Mr. Treet himself came into the parlor, beamed at his brood, and shook me warmly by the hand.

"Charmed to see you, dear George! Really charmed!"

"I've brought you something . . ."

"God bless you! And He will, I'm sure!"

I gave him the purse, which he dropped into his pocket out of sight of the landlord's painted eyes.

"There's a vessel sails on the noonday tide. Must go and see the captain. Back in five minutes . . ."

He was indeed—smiling gravely. The die was cast and the Treets were bespoken for lands across the sea.

"Mr. Dexter looks pale, don't you think, Father?" said Miss Treet, suddenly. Mr. Treet looked at me searchingly.

"Not pale but elegant, child," he explained. " 'Tis a more genteel complexion."

"He looks worried, Father," pursued Miss Treet, not satisfied.

"And not vastly happy . . ."

"Nonsense, child! He's rich, loved, secure, and hugely well-situated! Ain't that so, George!"

"Yes, indeed, Mr. Treet, sir."

"There, miss! What did I say! The world's at his feet. . . ."

"Could you not come away with us, Mr. Dexter?" asked Miss Treet, softly.

I smiled. "I've a family, Miss Treet."

"Like uth, George?"

"What *are* they like, Mr. Dexter? Your father . . . ?"

"Is handsome, dignified, and generous."

"And your mother?"

"Is—is—er—elegant, witty, and humorous."

"I think I'd prefer her. If she's really humorous."

"My father's been ill. . . ."

"Ain't there no more in your great house? For you mutht all rattle round like three peath in a great big drum!"

"Indeed, it sounds lonely, Mr. Dexter."

"Great gentlemen, child," pronounced Mr. Treet, "have no need of company to be content."

"That's true," said Edward, wisely. "For in all plays, accounts, and histories, they talk to themselves more often than to their families!"

Which remark led to all the Treets remembering a great many things that had no bearing on the present circumstance. Plays seen, places visited, places chased out of, great triumphs and small disasters, tremendous journeys, and a horse we once had called "Webster" who looked exactly like the Mayor of Rye . . . which was when Hotspur had been a snoozing infant.

"How strange it seems, Mr. Dexter, that you should remember we Treets even plainer than we remember ourselves!"

"And I'll not forget you, either. Not ever, Miss Treet!"

"Nor we you, George!" exclaimed Mr. Treet, suddenly upon his feet, for it was grown near departure time. "No matter what grandness the future holds, no matter what glories are to come—we'll think on you, George. Our thoughts will conquer oceans and mountains—and visit you in your comfort and quiet. We will never be quite parted, my boy!"

So the time was come. Already! Farewells were bright-eyed . . . even in the parlor's substantial gloom. But Mr. Treet's eyes were veiled and dreamy . . . and his round voice seemed to fill the room like a species of "Lucifer's Smoke."

"Come, Treets, away!"

Sadly, I watched them go out of the parlor and into the street, and the landlord's bulging black eyes swiveled after them, back and forth . . . one, two, three, four, five, six, seven—and they were gone.

I sat for, maybe, half an hour in the dull quiet, listening for the muffled harbor sounds: the grinding of chains, the creak of ropes, and the ancient shouts of sailors as sails tumbled down from yards and took their bellyful of the wind. Was that their vessel? In my mind's eye I saw the eternal parting of wood and stone, as the ship moved off from the quayside, and the gulf between—at first no wider than a hand—grew broad and deep as a wound, then stretched till all possible links were broke . . . and it was as if a whole world had gone adrift beyond all recall.

Mrs. Montague and her suspicions had been defeated. But at some little cost. The Treets were gone forever.

I went outside—and felt the landlord's eyes swivel after me too. (Did he never speak?) The street looked old and lonely—as I suspected it always did when a ship had just sailed . . . for everyone would have gone down to the harbor to wave and watch. There was a harsh screaming of seabirds in the air—a very melancholy sound.

"You are a monstrous old bag, Mrs. Montague—and as slimy a liar as your dead little gentleman underground! For I've lost my friends and it gives me no pleasure to've proved you wrong. For I knew in my heart all the time that Mr. Treet was an honest man!"

*   *   *

A loose bundle of humanity had come up some narrow stone steps that led down to a fisherman's beach. They kicked and scraped on the cobbles, and some scraps of sea mists seemed to be tangled among their feet—like they were a family of linen drapers, quarreling in muslin. . . . I stared at them.

The Treets! Come back! Not gone! One . . . two . . . three . . . four . . . five . . . six . . . seven! Mr. Treet himself! Waving! Smiling apologetically!

"Hullo there! George! Ha-ha! Imagine! We missed the ship! By a yard! I shouted—shook my fist! 'Captain! What of our seventy pound?' No reply! The wind took my words—and consequently, our capital! Ha-ha! We're back again, my boy! No need to look tragic! You've done handsomely—and we'll manage as before! What's a few pound between you and us? Nothing! Even less! For the Treets are onstage again!"

I rode back to Fulking at the head of a ghostly army: Colonel Suspicion, Captain Mistrust—and Sergeant Doubt. The ground seemed to be shifting from under my feet, and not all the "Lucifer's Smoke" in the world—be it thick as knitting wool—could have supported me long. For Mr. Treet had been proven no surer an anchor than my uncle in the copse. He'd shifted, gone adrift, and now moved in the dark with the rest of them. . . . Edward Treet's words haunted me. The Principal. He must be found—and dragged out into the light of day! For his sinister lurkings made everything sinister. . . . If he was not my uncle (and sometimes I thought he was, and sometimes I thought it to be impossible), then his quiet motions had made a monster where there'd been nothing more or less than an unlucky man. Likewise with my cousin, for they'd changed him from a peevish youth of no account into a cunningly murderous lout. And Mr. Treet—my Mr. Treet!—from a tremendous genius into a leech of the darkest intent! Oh! He'd have much to answer for, would that mysterious gentleman! But in whose voice would the answer come?

"Well, nephew—did you use the pistol?"

My uncle, standing by the road, in the shadow of the trees. I wondered if he'd taken root—for he seemed not to've moved since I'd left him.

I shook my head; footpads, thieves, and High Tobies seemed to've declared a holiday and gone to church though it was a Wednesday.

"Did you give your friend the money?"

I declined to reply—for it was none of his affair.

"And he didn't go?" said my uncle, perceptively. "Well, well—I'm sorry you've been disappointed. A spy in the camp is harder to face than a regiment on the field. My sympathies, nephew." He sighed. "But I wasn't waiting to hear that. I was waiting to change back pistols, child. For we don't want needless suspicion aroused. To go out with one pistol and come back with another might provoke too much interest. . . ."

We exchanged weapons, and I saw, more plainly this time, the undoubted damage to the barrel of the pistol I'd been given. Silently, we parted—he to the dark of the copse, and I toward the house.

After about twenty yards I fancied I heard him following me. I stopped—and turned. Something of a shadow seemed to've moved suddenly into concealment. I continued on my way. For five or six yards more. Then stopped again. And turned. Nothing. Yet "nothing" made some odd sounds among the fringing trees. But remained unseen. Yet my horse was restless—and shifted under me like a rough sea. I turned to go on.

"Move—and I'll blow yer head off!"

A Wednesday churchgoer. Left before the sermon. A gent in dark and dirty brown. Masked. Aiming a pistol the size of a cannon. A murderer if ever I saw one! Directly in my path! To spare me the trouble of doing so myself, my horse gave a scream of alarm! And began to back away—

"I warned you!" His pistol was wavering—searching out my head! Desperately, I reached for my own weapon—pulled it out—

I thought, for an instant, that it was he who'd fired, for the flash and roar were tremendously close at hand. Till I saw him clutch at his throat and drop to the ground!

My uncle, sweating like a pig, limped out of the trees.

"Saw him follow . . . by God! But you was nearly done for! Didn't you remember your weapon was stacked? Would have blown you to Hades without ever his assisting! By God! But it was close!"

The shot man was stirring—and moaning in an unpleasantly bubbly fashion, for his throat was opened to the air. My uncle bent down and pulled at his mask. A mean, pinched face—very deserving of a mask . . . more so than ever when dying.

"Only a joke . . . only a joke . . ." he mumbled.

He was gone in seconds. Upon his person was thirty pound in gold. My uncle took it—and told me to go back to the house and say nothing. He would bury the body. In the copse.

· 14 ·

WHEN I came in I was met by my father; he was gray-faced and trembling. He'd heard the shot and instantly dreaded that some mischief had befallen me! I thought of his "limping heart" (Dr. Newby's expression) and quickly disclaimed any danger and declared the shot to've come from far away.

"Thank God, thank God!" he muttered—and to hear him say that was a vastly warming thing. Indeed, on that cold afternoon and night, it was the *only* warming thing!

I thought hard and fearfully on that footpad with thirty pound in his ragged pocket. "Only a joke," he'd said. Who'd had so queer a sense of humor, then? Spending thirty pound and a life on the chance of raising a smile! Not Bertram—never Bertram! For thirty pound was right out of his world! And he'd shown no shock on seeing me. Only his ordinary displeasure. I asked him, even, if he was an authority on pistols, and he'd looked at me as if I was suddenly gone out of my mind. Unless he was a better actor than I (which was

impossible) he was as innocent as he was unpleasant—
and he couldn't have been more guiltless than that!

But I believed that someone *had* paid that luckless
man in the wood to waylay me in the hope I'd fire and
blow myself to bits.

Little by little I began to feel that dark events were
quickening—whirlpool-like—and I and all about me were
being drawn in . . . even sucked down to the heart of
that whirlpool where, black and huge, lurked the Principal himself . . . stirring, stirring with a long, red
spoon. . . . Which made me wish, with all my heart,
that I'd stayed in Shoreham with the Treets, frail as
their father had proven to be.

For I'll have you know, it was no very cheerful thing
to lie abed at night and consider that—under the same
roof, most likely—someone was engaged in devising
one's end. Even the best of us would sleep ill, get up a
dozen times in the night, then appear in the morning as
pale, bloodless, and hollow-eyed a ghost as if the murderer had already done his business and the household
was now observing its horrid result!

"He looks poorly," remarked my Aunt Dexter, with a
satisfied smile. "But then he always was a sickly child."

On which my mother coolly shrugged her shoulders
and made no answer. Nonetheless, during that same
morning, she would not let Dr. Newby leave till he'd
promised her my condition was not serious.

Which he did, but added that it would do no harm to
keep me within doors till the weather improved. This
was a favorite saying of his, for he was a firm believer in
the malice of the misty air. I think that, when he's dead
and summoned at last to Judgment, he'll keep cautiously to his coffin and answer:

"No, Sir! Not till the weather improves!"

But the only change in the weather seemed to be for the worse. An easterly wind set in, and, far from dispersing the mists the doctor dreaded, brought reinforcements from the sea. Great, ghostly battalions came rolling over the Downs: dirty muslin mountains . . . dark, threatening, secretive, hung against the sky in banked assemblages . . . then came down. . . .

The Captain, in the copse, must have been in wretched circumstances. I wondered if his friend, Mrs. Montague, had offered him shelter, but then certain items I heard suggested the lady was too cautious for that, and the Captain was foraging elsewhere. Pies, bread, and sausages were being pilfered from the Shepherd and Dog, and an outhouse had been slept in for two nights past. A kitchenmaid, coming by the copse at dusk, had seen a gaunt shape skulking among the silver trees . . . "like a tarnished fork." She'd shrieked and fled to save her soul—believing the scullery to be the securest place for it.

"Hunt him down!" demanded the landlord, believing him to be no more than a marauding vagrant, but the parson was for extending him the compliments of the season, and not winkling him out till Christmas was done.

"God rest you, hungry gentleman—
Till after Christmas Day!"

But once mentioned, the idea of the hunt took root. . . .

During that day, and the next, Joseph asked four times for my pistol to be returned to the gun room, saying my father was most particular over the sensible care of weapons. And four times I fobbed him off. If my father had seen the fatal damage, his "limping heart" would have stopped.

Meanwhile, the weather continued evil, and, on the Saturday, some sleety rain fell so's I felt pity enough for the man in the copse to think of taking him a coat. But a certain uneasiness made me reconsider. For the copse had a fresh occupant (though, as time passed, not so fresh as he'd been). The Captain was one matter; the corpse was quite another. For it would not have been buried deep—my uncle having nothing substantial to dig with. . . . Maybe it had only been covered with leaves? Quite possibly, for the Captain, being military, would be casual with corpses, while I, being brought up with geniuses, was no such thing.

On the same afternoon the hunt was mentioned for a second time, and fixed for the Tuesday, for the landlord had been newly bereaved of a lantern and a great pork sausage.

"He seems to be settling in for the winter, Mr. George, sir," said Joseph. "But Tuesday will see the end of him. For Sir John is a great huntsman. Fox, deer, hare, partridge, or vagrant! I'd not set any of their lives at a shilling's purchase!"

I thought, briefly, of going out to warn my thieving uncle that his principal prospect was of death or disfigurement . . . horror and shame . . . and that he'd best occupy the Christmastime till Tuesday in shifting his seedy self out of the copse—and out of the county too. Then again reconsidered—and hoped his friend, Mrs. Montague, would have warned him off.

The rain stopped, but the night was premature—on account of the thickness of the air—so that the sun gave up trying to reach us at about half after three. Dr. Newby, braving the weather, called again. He, too, had heard of the hunt, and positively forbade my father to take any part. My father laughed, and, glancing at me with a sudden, sly humor, asked the doctor if he'd never heard the principal danger was to the hunted, not to the hunter. The doctor sighed—and turned to me.

"My dear George, unless you've a strong mind to inherit directly, beg your father to avoid this hunt."

This was the first time Dr. Newby had voiced any new fears for my father's life. They came as a terrible shock.

"This—is he still dying, then?" I asked the doctor at the door.

"We are all dying," was the somber reply.

"I mean . . . are his days—numbered, sir?"

"*All* our days are numbered."

"But do you know . . . the number of *his*?"

"Only if he goes hunting on Tuesday, George. *Then* their number is three!"

"Does he know?"

The doctor stared at me and nodded. My heart contracted with anguish and pity. Much—indeed, almost all—of my father's changeability, his sometime coldness, his sometime boundless warmth, stood explained! A man to whom Death has sent up his card may well fidget in his soul. . . . During that night I swore to myself I'd force my uncle to quit the district before Tuesday. With no quarry there'd be no hunt.

But, on the morning of Christmas Eve, it became plain that my uncle had more of a stake in the copse than the nearness of the larder of the Shepherd and Dog. . . .

Mrs. Montague, in company with Parson Bennett, called to collect gifts for the poor of the parish. For which Christian charity, my mother gave me a guinea. . . .

"God bless you, Master Dexter!" cried Mr. Bennett.

"This will keep the wolf from a cottage door!" (Why was Mrs. Montague eyeing me so queerly . . . as if I was risen—mutinously—from the dead?)

"Oh no, sir!" I said, distractedly. " 'Tis for the cottager—not the wolf!"

Much laughter, of a forced kind . . . and more queer, even hostile, looks from Mrs. M. But she avoided speaking to me direct until she was leaving. And then she contrived to whisper:

"Something's been discovered! In the copse. You must go!"

I supposed her to've had some conversation with "Mister Only-a-Joke" in his private place in the wood. I stared at her, vastly alarmed.

"Well, child, will you come?"

"N-not till the weather improves, ma'am!"

She looked at me as if I was mad.

"An evil Christmas, Mr. George, sir," said Joseph, meaning the weather. "The worst in all my years here. But they say it'll clear up for the hunt."

God help me, but I *had* to go to the copse and plead with the wretched Captain . . . and tempt him away from his discovery—no matter what it was!

Joseph was rambling on—about past Christmases. Though none of them had been gay—by the standards of the Treets, that is—none of them had been as somber as this. Even in my grandfather's day, when Sir John and the Captain ("Never breathe his name!") had been young men. For the deep enmity between them had had its springtime then. If there'd been any love lost between them, it had been a very starved item, skinny enough to've fallen between the floorboards. . . . (There went my hopes of appealing to my uncle's sense of "flesh and blood!" From Joseph's air, the only way it would have been palatable to my uncle was if the blood had been spread on the flesh like jam!)

"But none so somber as this," finished up Joseph, with his gallows grin.

I reserved my visit to the copse for Christmas Day itself—and hoped that the spirit of peace and goodwill would have driven out some of the malevolence of that place. But before that, at dusk on Christmas Eve, I had a visitor.

"Mr. George, sir. A—a young lady. She'll not come in, but begs to see you. . . ."

It was Miss Treet! Jane!

She curtsied.

"Miss Treet! Please, come inside!"

She smiled and shook her head. Then she raised her hand—and out of the night itself came a chorus of amazing sweetness.

"God rest you merry, gentlemen.

Let nothing you dismay!"

And then they came, seeming to drift in from the very air and take their familiar shapes and dear faces, till they were a close-packed circle before me, with the porch lanterns lighting up their singing eyes and lips— the beloved Treets themselves!

I felt like weeping at the pleasure of their coming— for they'd come when my spirits were down. And, strangely enough, I longed very much for my mother to join me at the door and hear how the six geniuses sang to their one-time seventh. But no one joined me; though, afterward, my mother said she'd seen them from an upper window, and, she added with a sly smile, she'd not come down in case they proved unreal and vanished away before their song was done!

"Comfort and joy! Comfort and joy!" they pealed . . . one after another, then together, for an end.

"Merry Chrithmath, George!"

"Merry Christmas, Hotspur! And to you all!"

Miss Treet said, "We've brought you a gift, Mr. Dexter." (My heart sank, for, not expecting them, I'd got them nothing.) She curtsied again—and gave me a small parcel.

"May I open it?"

"Go on, George! Open it, pleathe!"

I did so. My eyes filled with tears. They'd given me something I'd never thought to possess, and had always longed for. God knows where they'd got it—or what it had cost! It was the most tremendous blue Steinkirk cravat with lace near a foot deep!

" 'Twill go handsome with your tabby waistcoat!" said Jane.

I begged them tell me where they were staying—so's I might send them presents. But Miss Treet shook her head.

"Though we're staying nearby—even at the Shepherd and Dog—our father bade us on no account to take more from you as you've already given so much!"

"But Jane—"

"One thing only he asks. He begs you visit him at the inn as soon as you may. For he's something of importance to confide."

It was then that a sudden chill struck my heart, and, helplessly, I wondered what it was that Mr. Treet wanted, that he didn't come to ask for himself? Another seventy pound? Or even more this time? Wretchedly, I avoided Jane's bright eyes.

"When will you come, Mr. Dexter? Please say—for our father is anxious."

"When the weather improves, Jane. I'll come when the weather improves."

On that same evening two neighbors called to discuss with my father the prospects for the Tuesday hunt. When they left he smiled at me and said:

"Well, boy—on Tuesday we'll see if I can teach you as shrewdly as Mr. Treet has done! He's taught you to be a man. I'll teach you to be a gentleman! Hmm! Or die in the attempt, eh? I'm sorry—sorry, boy! It's Dr. Newby! He's a gloomy specter for these Christmas days! So we'll cheer up, boy! Not so down in the mouth! For there's no tragedy but the weather! And they say that's improving!"

· 15 ·

THE WEATHER was improving. During the night the wind had changed, and the heavy sea mists had been bundling themselves up in a slow retreat. By morning the prospect from my window was clearer than ever I'd seen it since I'd come to the house.

But the change had come too late, for all our looked-for Christmas guests had cried off on account of the sinister weather . . . leaving us with nothing but a houseful of syllabubs, pies, cakes, and game—and enough white soup to float a man-of-war. It lay in a huge tureen that had been hoisted onto a sideboard in the great hall and steamed mournfully . . . sending its odors up to the painted martyr who hung above it, like a fresh torment to that much-abused man.

But then, during the morning, the cheerful Rumbolds sent a servant to say that they'd be happy to wait on her ladyship in the afternoon—if that would suit—for they still feared the evening and night would bring a return of the wretched weather. And this suddenly renewed prospect of Christmas visitors seemed to transform the

house entirely, so that the arrival of the Rumbolds—
though they were by no means to've been the chief of
the guests—was looked forward to with real pleasure
and excitement. Even the threat of the Tuesday hunt,
with all its dark, unnatural dangers, seemed less terrible, and I put off the necessary meeting with my uncle
in the copse till after the Rumbolds should have gone.

The only disagreeableness of the new arrangement
was that it prevented my taking presents to the Treets
at the inn that morning, on account of my mother
bidding me keep within the house lest the guests arrived before their time. Somewhat sadly, I wondered
what gifts bone-poor Mr. Treet would be providing for
his hopeful brood. Not that he was ever at a loss, for
there'd always been old trinkets of Mrs. Treet's for the
females, while his great imagination had never been
defeated by the rest of us. I smiled as I remembered
how he'd once given historical Edward an old Malmsey
bottle with three or four long sodden silken hairs in it
and sworn it had been drawn off the very butt the Duke
of Clarence had been drowned in! Oh! He'd a rare gift
for gifts!

But then, so had my mother, who'd given me a
handsome amethyst seal ring engraved with "G.D." It
was only my father who'd been unlucky, for he more
than any of us seemed to be the eternal victim of the
evil Principal, who subtly warped his actions and ate
out his heart. With the best will in the world he'd given
me—the worst thing in the world! Through Joseph,
he'd bade me keep the finely chased pistol I'd seemed
so fond of that I'd not wanted to be parted from. And
wished me well to use it—on the morrow's hunt!

And yet this ill-fated gift of his made me feel warmer
toward him than if he'd given me a new curricle and a

dappled mare! For it had shown a kindly understanding and an amiable regard. He must have inquired what his son was partial to; most likely he'd asked Joseph, and Joseph had told him, that of all things, I'd seemed most fond of the borrowed pistol—for four times I'd avoided giving it back!

The unconscious horror of the gift—with its silent invitation for me to blow my head off—was the cruelest thing the Principal had brought about . . . and it filled me with a sense of outrage that died down only after the Rumbolds had arrived.

For, next to the Treets, I think I was more pleased to see them than any other family in the land! Out of their carriage and into the house they came with the uproar of an invading army, for the Rumbold children—their cheeks much cherried by the wind—were in a state of high excitement, having been promised God knew what marvels and sweets and gifts on the way to prevent their jumpings about oversetting the coach!

"Oh, ma'am!" panted Mrs. Rumbold, as her cloak was took and her gown opened out like a cabbage. "I hope Sir John don't take their racket amiss! But they're so happy to've come, after being told that they wasn't, that the journey was one long fright and palpitation! How d'ye do, ma'am!" (This to my Aunt Dexter, who was laced so tight that she creaked like a new harness.)

Then Mr. Rumbold shook hands with me and my Newgate cousins and went off with a sigh of relief to talk with my father and Dr. Newby . . . leaving his lady to go frantic after their children, who, she was sure, would pull the house down if they wasn't watched and scolded for every single minute.

But it wasn't so much their running about the hall, climbing on and off chairs and banging the great tureen

(when they'd discovered it made a prosperous noise)—
for in their home they were given as much freedom
as their dogs—that nearly did for the house—it was
their dancing!

Our housekeeper played the harpsichord and the
Rumbold children performed with the thump and thunder of a hundred-gun broadside! Not a word was spoke
between them as they footed it—for they were scowling
with concentration to get their steps right. And every
movable item in the hall rattled and shuddered in alarm.
Even the Newgate Dexters (clumsy as they were) moved
like Italians by comparison . . . and Mrs. Montague
(who had been the first to arrive, in a festive black)
stood up with Edmund Dexter, and danced like a fat
black clump of thistledown.

I danced with my mother, who, once her first awkwardness and stiffness from long neglect had worn off,
moved with a really wonderful grace. She was, indeed,
a better dancer than Jane Treet, having a natural dignity in all her movements that made one want to stand
back and admire. But I was determined to equal her,
and so well did she judge the music that I was able to
double and redouble my steps—and even execute small
leaps—without the smallest inconvenience.

"Vagabond!" I heard Bertram Dexter, who clumped
with my aunt, mutter (—*he* had feet like monuments!)

Once or twice I looked to catch my father's eye, but
he always seemed engrossed by Dr. Newby and so
missed the best of my efforts.

But my greatest pleasure didn't come from the dancing. It came from the Rumbolds' delight on seeing me
again and recalling the best of our last meeting. For, in
their memories, my performance in their parlor had

been multiplied and magnified till they could talk of nothing else.

They poured out their admiration to everyone they could find: to Mrs. Montague, to the Newgate Dexters—who, with the exception of Bertram, took it amazingly well—to Dr. Newby, who looked interested, to my mother, who reminded them that she knew . . . and to my father.

"Have you seen George Dexter as Prince Hal?"

"Have you seen George Dexter as Mark Antony?"

"Have you seen George Dexter as General Othello? The way he dies!"

"A real Davy Garrick you've got there, Sir John!" said Mr. Rumbold to my father, who raised his eyebrows and nodded. (I fancied he thought Mr. Rumbold was praising me up to please him—for at that time he'd no real notion of my quality.)

In short, the Rumbolds were my slaves, and their children followed me everywhere I went for tales of my adventures in the wagon with Otway and the Treets, and once told, they'd rush off and relate them to everyone else, much enlarging them as they did so.

Not that I was offended, as, for the first time in the house of my birth, I felt I was a person of consequence, and an object of pride to my parents.

"But your fine clothes!" cried Mrs. Rumbold. "What's become of 'em? Ah! We was all looking forward to it! The children no more than me!"

"Yes, indeed!" cried several little Rumbolds. "*Please* why ain't you like the prince you was? For 'tis Christmas!"

"Yes, indeed, young man! We was expecting it! For shame, Sir John—and your ladyship too—to hide so gay a jewel in the dark!"

I can't tell you how strong was the happiness I felt! I

could scarcely believe that these good people could have wrought such a change! Even Bertram Dexter contrived—in my excited eyes—to look almost agreeable!

I made my hurried excuses and flew to my room—to the chest I'd always known I'd be opening at just such a time as this. Out they came! King Charles's green coat! Othello's yellow tabby waistcoat with its rich silver lace! The stockings with "bas de soye shot through!" The white silk breeches! The red-heeled shoes worn by a Marshal of France! Even the grand Dutch wig with its two tails and great black bow . . . and last and most handsome of all, the blue Steinkirk cravat with its foot-deep border of lace!

Off went my dull clothes and on went my glory, till I shone like the rising sun! There was nothing of me— even to the tips of my fingers (scrubbed till pink)—that wasn't of the finest and most princely!

Then down the stairs I went and fairly burst upon the great hall with " 'Friends, Romans, countrymen!' "

And how they cheered and clapped! For this time, with their goodwill at the outset, I gave them a performance they'd never forget!

Comedy, tragedy, drama, and passion! Not just fragments, but whole scenes! For many of the most excellent pieces are not writ for one performer, but need interjections, such as "Truly!" "Indeed!" " 'Tis strange!" to prick the course and whip it on. So I took all parts, shifted here and there, altered my voice, my stature, my whole person to give a rare richness . . . missed nothing . . . gave everything! (And, every now and then, stole a sly, satisfied look at my mother, who was deeply entranced, and then, proudly, to my father, whose eyes never left me. . . .)

"General Othello! General Othello!" screamed the

Rumbold children as I ended each scene. For that performance had made the deepest impression. So at last, and to signify the end, I begged a fruit knife and began upon that stupendous farewell in which the mightiest passions in the universe flare up, blaze—then flicker and die.

" 'I kissed thee ere I killed thee, no other way but this,
Killing myself, to die upon a kiss.' "

I staggered, sank—half recovered, then knelt . . . seemed to crawl toward something precious . . . then groaned, twitched—and died!

Silence. The most absolute silence. I dared not move for seconds so's not to break the spell. My head being buried in my sleeve (to this day, I can still recall a rough edge of braiding pressing against my cheek), I could see nothing.

Then I heard someone begin to clap . . . loudly, slowly, evenly. I looked up. Everyone was staring at my father. He was on his feet. And clapping. But not with much joy. His face was pale—gray, almost—so's I wondered briefly if his heart was to blame.

"A farewell indeed!" he said—and tried to smile, though nothing was further from him!

Then he went on, staring everywhere but at me, as if the sight of me, half kneeling on my imaginary stage, was deeply humiliating to him. He said . . . I cannot exactly recall his words, for I felt a sudden sickness and shame and a deep desire to be forgot . . . he said—and I believe he was striving to be gentle against his anger—he said that much must be forgiven me on account of my upbringing. And that my understanding of what was seemly was to be judged by—by other standards.

"Good friends, what appears lofty in the players' booth

unluckily seems coarse, vulgar, and ridiculous when seen so close as this! So do not judge him harshly. He knew no better. But now he does . . . and—and it injures *me* to see him injured in your eyes. So—so we'll let his unlucky past die, as he says, upon a kiss. Come to me, boy!"

In a maze of horrible, unbelieving shame, I began to stand up . . . when, with a quick, abrupt rustle, my mother left her place and came to my side.

" 'No other way but this!' " she murmured—and, bending slightly, kissed my brow!

I saw my father stare at my mother profoundly. The only other face I remembered was that of Bertram Dexter. I saw his lips move and form the word "Vagabond." I never, in all my life, saw anyone look so monstrously pleased.

Somehow or another—whether I was told, or went of my own accord, I can't remember—I climbed to my room and changed my shining clothes . . . for to lay them in what to me was their coffin.

Then, after a while, I returned downstairs . . . and was relieved to discover the Rumbolds and Mrs. Montague to've gone. Likewise, the Newgate Dexters were not to be seen. My father alone remained in his place, looking unbelievably weary. . . .

"I'm sorry, sir," I said.

He shook his head. "Indeed. I know. We are both sorry. But we must forget. We must forget this day."

He sighed—then took me by surprise by extending his hand for me to shake, and murmuring:

"Is it a bargain, boy?"

"A bargain, sir."

"Then the past's dead. Only tomorrow remains. Tomorrow, boy. The hunt. That's what I've in mind for you! Tomorrow! That's what we both long for, eh?"

At that moment Dr. Newby—who'd been in a high-backed chair and had so been invisible—jumped up and declared:

"I've warned you, Sir John! I'll not be answerable!"

"And to whom *should* you be answerable, sir?" demanded my father, with spirit. "For I'll tell you—if I'm to be robbed of all pleasures and pride, then my life's not worth the keeping!"

He turned back to me. "Boy—the hunt. You and me. Tomorrow!"

· 16 ·

MY HATRED for the Principal was, by this time, pretty strong, for every present disaster, misery, and uncanny danger had its roots in his act of thirteen years ago. A very lurid flower that was now in its full season.

I left for the copse at about four o'clock, when the sun was setting in a great commotion, and sending tremendous black shadows across the terrace and drive. I was much burdened with thoughts, least among which was my coming meeting with the seedy fellow in the wood.

The prospect of being a gentleman seemed as comfortable as the weather—which was bitterly cold. Still, I supposed, like the serpent, I'd grow another skin—and, in years to come, be as cool and scaly a Dexter as ever sat in a gilded frame . . . and stared, and smiled, and stared again. The grandeur and folly of my past life seemed as remote as the sun itself, which was now all but slipped into a pocket between two hills and looked no more than a coiner's clipping.

And yet—and yet it seemed harsh to believe that the Rumbolds hadn't been honest in their admiration. . . . A frail hope began to flicker . . . a hope that, sometime in the future, when I'd mastered the accomplishments that were demanded of me, when I and the house were one, when my father should be satisfied that the "boy" was worthy to be called "son"—*then* I'd open up that chest again, blow off the dust, alarm the moths, put on my bright clothes, and show my father that I could still play more parts than one!

But in the meantime, I'd remember that a gentleman don't wear his heart in his hat. He wraps it up and puts it, safe and sound, in an old oak chest.

I stopped and turned to look back at the house, which now bulked black against a bruised and bloody sky. And yet, with lights shining in several windows, it looked oddly threadbare. . . .

I must have been very deep in thought at that time— for I never heard a carriage approaching till it was almost on me! With a cry of alarm, I hopped out of the way, and it thundered past.

It was a squarish coach of the build that's never out of fashion by never being in it. Not a country coach—too precipitately driven for that. Despite everything else in my mind, I'd room enough to wonder what was the urgency of the errand that had brought the coach and its invisible occupant (for I saw nothing of him save a dead white hand resting on the window sash) out so late on Christmas Day?

Maybe it was some traveler who'd lost his way? Then why hadn't he stopped at the inn, which he must have passed? No, no lost traveler, him. And, in my alarmed state, I wondered if his thundering past had been another attempt upon my life.

"George, George! You're seeing more villains now than even would Joseph! A lost traveler, that's all. He must have missed the inn."

I turned away, shrugged my shoulders—and went into the copse.

"Who—are—you?"

Thus a queerly intent, shawled-up Mrs. Montague humped in the clearing.

The light was almost gone, and the stolen lantern (the landlord of the Shepherd and Dog would have been pleased to know), for economy's sake, was turned low. So the lady had not been able to make me out clearly, and said again:

"Who—are—you?"

"Not a ghost, ma'am, but George Dexter."

My uncle was sat on his tree stump, and, I saw with pity and shame, he'd stole the dead man's old brown cloak and was wrapped in it. He and his companion seemed suddenly lonely and forlorn—he with nothing but a dead man's rags to keep him warm . . . and she with nothing but dead men's lies to keep her company. . . .

I felt brutish—landlordish, even—adding to my uncle's misery by telling him to begone, but then considered that, if he stayed, his misery would be added to even more substantially. I was wondering how I might soften the blow . . . when he said:

"I was digging our friend of Wednesday's grave, you know . . ."

"He was digging a grave . . ." muttered Mrs. Montague, "when he found—another!"

"I'd nothing much to dig with, you see." (He never moved as he spoke . . . and his dark shape had an oddly guilty air.) "So I looked for where the earth was soft."

"It had been dug before," said Mrs. Montague.

"Not two foot down," went on my uncle, "working with a knife and my bare hands . . . in the dark, you understand . . . with our Wednesday friend alongside . . . ha! ha! Like I was a humble sapper and him the dozing sergeant!"

"When he came upon the pitiful remains of—of a child!" whispered Mrs. Montague.

Suddenly, my uncle stood up—and I'd a fearful sensation that all the trees in the copse stood up with him . . . and that he was about to show me that old grave with its young inhabitant, or worse, that—all unknowing—he was crouching on it, as if to batten it down! For the immediate ground—all ragged in the lantern's mean light—looked everywhere freshly dug, and scarce filled in!

"D-do you know . . . who the child was?"

Needless question. From Mrs. Montague's profound eyes and thin black line of a mouth the answer stood plain. The child was the dead little gentleman!

The copse was cold, dark, and had a grim smell. Scarce any mists remained—and such as did (seen curiously in the lantern light) were low and still, like starved white worms that had perished among the roots of the trees. Mrs. Montague kept staring at me, like I'd done her an ancient wrong. . . .

"The remains of a child . . . an infant of no more than a year."

" 'Tis not certain, ma'am," interposed my uncle.

"Don't change your tack, Mr. Richard—for you and I have thought deep about it."

I asked again. "Then who was the child?"

"The question is, Master George—who are *you*?"

"George Dexter!"

"Indeed? Then who lies in the grave?"

"Why—God knows!"

"For why should a year-old child be buried secretly? Why should his death be hid? Why not in the church-yard? Why here, in this copse? So near the house! Can you answer that, Master George? Do you, maybe, know more of this than you'd care to say? Is there a secret in your heart?"

"He's innocent!" declared my uncle. "That I'll swear to! Whatever's the truth, he don't know it!"

"Oh my God! What are you talking of? What d'you suspect?" (My voice sounded tipsy with dismay.)

"That you and the little dead one are much con-cerned with each other . . . even in each other's pocket."

My hands, which had been in my coat pockets, came out directly, for such was the grimness of the lady's tone that I was sharply alarmed that I'd meet with thin, questing bone.

"A child stolen," went on Mrs. Montague, "from the house—a child of a year. A child found in this copse—a child of, maybe, a year. Thirteen years after the theft a youth appears, put forward as the pilfered child. He has—or, rather, his putter-forward has the infant's cloth-ing . . . and certain other things besides. George Dex-ter? Maybe . . . maybe. But the odds are not so strong. For who is the dead little one? What if the dead child was George Dexter? Then who are you?"

Her voice, though low, crackled and grated like an old chain, gripping link by link. . . .

"What if tiny, sickly George Dexter perished when he was stole . . . or, what if he was murdered? Murdered by his thief! And another child substituted—for the enormous gain of claiming the great inheritance?"

Her suspicion was as plain and ugly as her face.

"You mean—Mr. Treet?"

"Who else? What if Mr. Treet had a son at that time? And you are that son to whom he now applies, time and again, for more and more money? Money from his own secret son? For the ties of flesh and blood are strong! So it turns out that the dead child who wept and cried to me all these years was George Dexter indeed!"

"Never! Never in ten thousand years! Mr. Treet would never have harmed a living soul! Not even a landlord—let alone a baby! He's too great a man for that! You're mad, Mrs. Montague! And you, my Uncle Dexter, had best begone! And take that dead little gentleman with you—to bear you company to the ends of the earth! Mr. Treet a murderer and burier of babies? Oh God! I could laugh at it was it not so wild, black, and vile!"

"I told you so," said my uncle, wearily. "I warned you, ma'am, you'd turn him against us by a false suspicion."

He heaved himself off his tree stump and limped up beside me.

"Look at it this way, my lad. There's more to this than meets your eye or mine . . . even this good lady's. Much respect to you—much honor, even—for defending your old friend. But there's certain questions he might answer was they put to him direct. Not that I subscribe to this lady's suspicions. I have my own."

"Mr. Richard! I forbid you to talk of them!" (Mrs. Montague—sharp as a pin!)

"All right, ma'am . . . but I know—what I know. And am better qualified . . . flesh and blood, ma'am . . .

"Look at it this way, George. Set aside the past and

consider the present. There's someone who's trying to shovel you underground, viz, the pistol and our Wednesday friend. (For he was no regular footpad, I'll swear!) Why? This good lady's suspicions don't answer that one! No, my boy. But mine do! Oh, George! It ain't for nothing I've knocked about in dark and desperate company these past dozen years! I know—I know—I know!"

"That company's twisted you, Mr. Richard—and soured you like bitter aloes!"

The cold was biting through to my bones, but it was warmer than my blood, which stood frozen in every part of me. What were my uncle's suspicions? And how were they more horrible than Mrs. Montague's?

"Mrs. Smith!" I whispered, suddenly desperate for anything these two opposed demons had forgot. "The nurse! Surely she'd know something . . . ?"

"Dead," said Mrs. Montague, queerly pleased to've stopped me. But what if she was dead, I thought. No problem to madam. Surely she could have called up a perished nursemaid to squeak in her sepulcher of an ear? But I didn't care to mention it. Instead, I tried elsewhere.

"The Stranger! Who was he? For surely he'd know?"

"Yes, indeed," said my uncle. "The Stranger. I fancy he'd have the answer to everything. The Stranger. Who do we know, ma'am, who has the answer to everything? My suspicions could point—but yours are void, ma'am. Confusion and defeat! My suspicions answer all! I can see . . . yes, I can dream what happened, and what is happening, and why—God help me!—even, I can see what will happen. But, damnation! Suspicion can't prevent it! George, George! Watch yourself, boy! For your danger is huge—and from a terrible source. Then why don't I tell you? No reason, save I may be mistook. And then—and then . . ."

He shivered and stood up. "Have you the damaged pistol still?"

I showed it to him . . . for I never left that deadly object behind.

"Then give it to me and take back its twin. You must have means of defense. Though I pray to God there'll never be the need!"

Silently we exchanged weapons—or I thought we did, for my brain was shaking and spinning so wildly that I was no longer sure of anything—save that I wished the night would turn warmer and my two companions would vanish through a hole in the ground. Then, dimly, I remembered why I'd come.

"The hunt. Tomorrow. They're going to hunt you down."

My uncle said, "Does *everyone* join this hunt?"

"Yes."

"Then beware. Look to your right. Look to your left. And look behind. For it may not be me who's being hunted."

When I reached the house the coach that had passed me was standing by the door. In my present state it could have been perched on the chimneys and I'd not have been amazed. Too much evil-smelling water had flowed under the bridge since last I'd seen it for me to care if it was Gabriel himself calling—with long brass coaching horn to blow a fine Last Trump.

When I was but twenty yards off the door opened and someone stepped quickly out and up into the coach. I saw nothing of him but his clothing—which, in the lamplight, was black. The coach started off—and I stepped to one side. This time I saw more of the occupant. I saw his papery, dead-white face.

Joseph was in the doorway.

"Why, Mr. George, sir—you're white and shaking! Pray to God you haven't took a chill! For it's that—or you've seen a ghost!"

"Joseph! Who was the—the gentleman in the coach?"

"Why, Mr. Craddock, Mr. George, sir. The lawyer."

"Where was he going?"

"To the inn, Mr. George, sir. He's staying at the inn."

I shuddered to the depths of my soul. For the man in the coach had been the Stranger!

· 17 ·

I SAW him on the terrace, just after two o'clock in the morning: Mr. Treet. There was a good moon, so I saw him well. The urgency to confide had drawn him out of his snug bed to skulk on the pale, cold terrace for a glimpse of me. Save Mr. Treet wasn't capable of skulking. There was a portliness about him that prevented. He tiptoed sharply back and forth, beetled neatly after by his shadow.

"Psst! George! Psst! George!"

I heard him, even through the shut window. Then a noise alarmed him and he darted to the concealment of the wall. I noticed he was wearing new silver shoe buckles—for they twinkled as he ran. . . .

A minute later he was out again, whispering more softly—for I heard nothing, but saw his lips move fishily. Several times he looked up to the windows, but the reflected moon must have hid me, for, in a little while, he went away. I felt no urge to join that false man.

I thought he'd given up for the night and was retired to bed. But he'd another notion. Truly remarkable. Of a sudden, I thought the copse had exploded! There was an orange sunburst, followed by billowy clouds of white—thick as knitting wool! The whole copse looked like it was dissolving in the rich vapor that seemed to pour out of every nook and cranny of its substance! It was extraordinary the whole house wasn't awake and gaping. But the phenomenon had been silent. It had only been Mr. Treet trying to draw my attention with a sample of "Lucifer's Smoke." Mercifully, the trees were dripping with damp, so they never took fire, and the wonder of the Treets slowly sank and died. God knew what my hidden uncle had imagined! That the dead had at last awakened—angry at being maligned?

Six hours to the hunt. Dr. Newby's warning haunted me. Was my father's time so short? And—was he my father? And that cool, pale, ironical lady . . . was she my mother? Besides God, who knew? The Stranger . . . Mr. Craddock. And he'd gone to the inn. Been with Mr. Treet. A conspiracy? Who apter than a lawyer? Maybe the estate had been pilfered to the bone and Mr. Craddock was in default up to his stringy neck? Together with Mr. Treet. What evil brew had they cooked up between them?

Dismal thoughts, like hungry beggars, kept pushing in. One was more monstrous and pocky than all the rest. What if that dead little gentleman had been an infant Treet? What if Mr. Treet had stole the Dexter and slaughtered his own child so's not to've come with one and gone with two? To avoid suspicion.

A very plaguey thought, that. I felt a chill of horror at having admitted it. To charge—even in the dark of my mind—a man who'd always seemed great, kind, and mostly good, with an act so dismal, wretched, and foul! Hmm! Yet such acts are performed—and men perform them. And, till they're found out, the presumption is the men are good. For every man's innocent till proven evil. And proof, like a faithful, slavering hound, must follow on the heel of suspicion. Without suspicion where can proof find a kennel? Nowhere—and never. Till, maybe, after death. I think hell must be vastly full of gentlemen surprising to all but themselves!

How many hours to the hunt? No sense in looking, for the number would be either too many—or too few.

Come, now! Christmas thoughts: Whitewash Mr. Treet for me and make him once more the grandly handsome genius, overflowing with quality! Or scour out my mind of everything and let me start afresh. For this is horrible—to be driven to think so ill of so many . . . when maybe only one deserves it! George Dexter! (But maybe not George Dexter?) George Treet, then! (But maybe not George Treet?) George! Ah! At least I'm George—and devil take the tailpiece! George! Yes, George? Oh—oh—I'd forgot what I wanted to say . . . so much to'ing and fro'ing of Treet and Dexter, that my brain's in a whirl with it! No matter! George is George—and that's me. There—in the secret place of my heart. George. What's he like, then, this deep, proud George? Ah! That would be telling! Indeed? Then Mrs. M. was right, and you have a secret?

"Mr. George, sir—I'm bidden to remind you we set out at eight, and 'tis now half after seven."

Extraordinary! Joseph already? So I'd slept? Got into bed and fallen asleep? I swear I never remembered doing so!

"Mr. George, sir . . ."

"I'm awake, Joseph."

"It's a fine day, Mr. George, sir. The weather's improved most miraculous. Scarce enough mist anywhere to hide so much as a hare—let alone a murdering vagrant!"

A breakfast of ale and sausage and pie—with a gill of brandy to keep out the cold. Then a second gill to soothe the first, which had quarreled with the sausage and gave me no peace.

"I wish you a pleasant morning, George—if you can find pleasure in such things."

Thus my mother—if she was my mother . . . if not, my Lady Dexter, looking briefly concerned.

"So pale and sweaty? Have you a fever?" She touched my head with her hand. "No. Cold . . . quite cold. But take care, George. Do not distress me by taking an injury or a chill. For I cannot abide being distressed."

"Indeed, he looks sickly, ma'am. The color of a peeled egg."

Thus my Aunt Dexter—or, if not, plain Mrs. Dexter, late of Newgate and no connection at all.

"Is he ready, madam? Has he eaten a hearty breakfast? Ah! He looks a credit to us! Not so—um—splendid as yesterday . . . but fine enough! Dressed to kill, eh, madam? Come, boy—let's be off!"

My father—or, if not, august Sir John Dexter, handsomely coated and flushed with excitement. For he'd not hunted for close on a year. He looked so gay and full of life that I was certain Dr. Newby had been mistook. But that glum physician's face appeared at my father's elbow like one of the grim little cherubs in old paintings who come to pluck out souls: vastly concerned; vastly troubled; vastly in dismay.

We were to meet with our neighbors on the other side of the copse, which we of the house were to scour first. For my father would not have that ancient and particular place turned into a "common stamping ground." And we were bidden to remember that, though our quarry might be murderous, we were not. We were to shoot at his legs—not at his head or his heart. For he was a man—not a beast of the forest or field.

"So you must shoot careful, Mr. George, sir," said Joseph. "And take an aim thus." He held up an imaginary pistol and sighted with his eye almost to where the hammer would have been. "For that's what I'm bidden to say. . . ."

I thanked him somberly. Shrewd advice to one who might too easily have had another weapon. (My head would have been wrapped round the air like a bloody snowstorm.) He moved away before I could ask him (if I dared) who'd given him such advice to pass so exactly on. (The Principal and me were drawing together. . . .)

We were only five on the terrace—the three Newgate Dexters, my father and me . . . for Dr. Newby, though asked and in the house, would not hunt. Though the sun was brilliant and the sky of a fine, wintry blue, the weather, it seemed, was not improved enough for the doctor to endure it. He would not venture into the copse. There was perniciousness and malice in it yet that might prove fatal. . . .

At eight o'clock we left the terrace and began to move across the lawn, spreading out into a long line. A Dexter rake, with five prongs. I wondered if my uncle was watching as his brother, his nephew, and his three sons came on to maim him.

My father signaled Bertram to move farther off, and not close up the agreed distance . . . for that scowling, sullen youth had tended to shift in—as if uneasy at entering the copse so far from company.

The shadow of the trees struck cold. I saw my father shudder with it—and called to him to button his coat, for it was flapping loose, like a pair of great, broken wings.

"Keep your eyes ahead, boy. Don't look to me."

But my uncle had said, "Look to your right. Look to your left. And look behind." What was behind me? The house. The terrace. A group of servants, waving us on. My mother—or was she my mother? My aunt—or was she my aunt?

My stomach began to bubble again like a witch's cauldron. Had I been poisoned at breakfast?

"Keep your eyes ahead, boy!" shouted my father—for we were entering the copse. "There's a murderer loose in here!"

The air smelled damp and rotten with decayed herbs, and the sun, striking through the bone-work of branches, made a sharp black net that, in a curious way, seemed to impede movement, though it was insubstantial. . . . "Look to your right. Look to your left." Nothing. I could see nothing, now, save the close-grown trunks of the birches, worked here and there with complicated ferns. I could hear my companions—but could not see them. . . .

The sickness which had been with me since I took the brandy came and went like a bailiff, impounding my very vitals. Either poison—or uncommon fear. Suddenly I saw Bertram, moving intently to my left. What was he doing so close? Then he saw me. And went gray with terror. Why? Abruptly, I realized I was pointing my pistol at him. He stared at it wildly—then blundered off out of sight.

I waited five minutes, ten minutes, then moved on—as cold, sick, fearful, dismal, and persecuted a fourteen-year-old as ever lived—and was likely to stop doing so at any moment. I watched the undergrowth; I watched the branches; I watched the black spaces between the trees. But not for any imaginary vagrant. I watched them for the Principal!

"Mrs. M.," I breathed. "If the Devil's in charge today—then here I come! But I warn you—I'll make a dull ghost, for I've a deal of sleeping to catch up on and will snooze underground for at least a year!"

"Psst! George!"

On my right! The stout, now sinister shape of Mr. Treet! What was he doing here? His coat was plucked at, his wig pulled, and his face scratched. But his eyes were glittering.

"Psst! George!"

I seemed to see him against a backcloth of treachery, avarice, and deceit. And it fitted him to a tee.

"Scoundrel!" I muttered bleakly . . . and shifted quickly on.

"George—George! Wait for me! George!"

I heard him following . . . then he seemed to take a wrong turn, for the sound of him dwindled, as did his plaintive cries of "George!" I halted for a moment . . . heard some sounds ahead . . . then went on as soft and quiet as to the forest born. Which brought me on something frightful, for my approach was unsuspected.

"You vile, contemptible animal!" I heard a voice mutter. "That thirty pound will cost you dear! You never crossed his path! The boy never laid eyes on you!"

The place was the clearing. Captain Dexter was crouched on his tree trunk, head shaded under the dead man's hat, form hidden in the dead man's cloak. The dead man of Wednesday. The one-time possessor of thirty pound. For which poor wretch the Captain had been mistook. By Sir John Dexter!

Which great gentleman stood at the opposing edge of the clearing, clutching at a tree for support in his freezing anger. I moved—and he saw me (but from what he said, it was plain he did not think I'd overheard him, and so thought himself still unsuspected).

"Ah! Boy! Good, good! There he is! Shoot, boy—shoot before he 'scapes! Quick, boy! Kill him! Aim, boy! Hold the weapon up! To your eye! Kiss the hammer, boy! Then fire! Fire, boy! Fire! I command you to fire!"

I stared at the terrible pallor of his face on which burned two spots of excitement—like prospects of hellfire. *The Principal!* He was the Principal—

"You're mad, brother John. You ought to be in Bedlam!"

The Captain had stood up. His voice was harsh with fear and shame and pity. Flesh and blood? His flesh must have crawled—and his blood curdled . . . as did mine . . . my God! As did mine!

Sir John was glaring. He clutched at his chest. I thought his heart had limped to its last halt. I think he dreaded the same. His face was panic-stricken. Then it changed—for his powerful spirit elbowed death aside. For the moment.

"You! Always you!"

He must have screamed those words—for they were heard to the limits of the wood, and brought a sound of running. The panic in his eyes had changed to hatred. "You!" he repeated—then flung himself violently upon his brother. This action was so sudden, powerful, and amazing that the Captain was overbalanced. He fell— and the madman seized up his weapon—that murderously damaged pistol that should have been mine—

"No! No! For God's sake, don't shoot, sir!"

He was aiming directly at my head. His face was now strained . . . more like the martyrs in the great hall than the Dexters who flanked them. His soul must have been full of arrows.

"It gives me . . . no joy to . . . kill you! But I must. You—are—not—my—son. O God. Never! Never! Never! You were destroying me! I—I could not live in you . . . too coarse, too bright, too strong! Maybe, had you been—otherwise, we'd not have come to this?"

"John! For God's sake! The pistol!"

"Don't shoot, sir—"

I fancy he thought I was begging for my life, for, the last I saw of them, his lips were vaguely contemptuous. Then he pulled the trigger. . . .

He did not die directly . . . but several minutes afterward, and in some confused pain. But when Dr. Newby came (fetched by Edmund), he was dead, and all the doctor was able to estimate was that the injuries he'd sustained, frightful though they were, would not have killed him unaided. The malignant condition of his heart, the doctor was certain, had been the true cause of his final destruction.

He was carried back to the house by Joseph and another servant. Joseph was crying like a child.

They laid him in the room where first I'd seen him . . . and on the same couch.

Captain Dexter accompanied his brother, and, with some dignity, withdrew from his wife's loud exclamations. For he took it as his duty to keep with the widow . . . Lady Dexter . . . my one-time mother, for I was George Treet—most likely—and was claimed by Mr. Treet, who never left my side, and never stopped telling me who I was—and had indeed been desperate to tell me for three days past. ("Why didn't you come to the inn, my dear?")

I saw Mrs. Montague, divided between shock at the frightful death, and pleasure at having been partly right. The dead little gentleman had been George Dexter—most likely—and had not lied. Henceforth she could trust the dead to the grave.

With amazement I saw it to be no later than half-past nine o'clock. It seemed not possible that, an hour and a half ago—because of one man's life—the world had been so vastly different a place. The air, the house, the silver birch copse itself, seemed now somewhat clear and still, with the brightness of a toy, inhabited by quiet ladies and gentlemen shrunk to a small proportion.

John, Edmund, and Bertram Dexter kept with their mother, murmured quietly from time to time—and glanced modestly from floors to walls to ceiling . . . then out to a view of the park. Captain Dexter was now with Mr. Treet and me . . . saying nothing save the oddest trivialities, such as, would we care for refreshment? Or, was not the weather turned fine? Dr. Newby had come down from Lady Dexter's bedroom—having given her a strong draught to compose her—and was mouthing all his secrets in Mrs. Montague's ear.

Even the flat, brown Dexters on the walls looked withdrawn and somewhat shrunk . . . like actors, after a performance, standing for their applause . . . smaller, tawdrier, and queerly less real than in the parts they'd filled in the play.

Parson Bennett came—acquainted with nothing save Sir John's death—and offered condolences. . . . Joseph, alone, was nowhere to be seen, for he was sitting with Sir John . . . and would not leave him till Mr. Craddock came. Which grim, papery-faced gentleman—yellowing somewhat at the edges—did indeed come at about quarter to eleven o'clock . . . and brought some whiffs of the old world with him. His first act was to go directly to the quiet room and fix his old, crabbed eyes on the canceled body of his dead Principal.

"His heart was diseased," murmured Dr. Newby.

"Indeed?" Mr. Craddock spoke dryly. "The cause of demise is your concern. The effect is mine. Pray tell Sir Richard Dexter I am at his service."

The Principal was dead. Long live the Principal. He closeted himself with the Captain for about an hour, during which time Dr. Newby mentioned often that "the heart was diseased, you see. . . . I told him some months ago . . . he'd not very long . . . that was certain . . . and I think you'll agree—if you examine carefully— that desperation followed on this knowledge . . . for, before it, though never of an outgoing nature, he was a calm gentleman of some contentment."

"He was never that, Dr. Newby, sir."

Joseph had come quietly into the room, his eyes soiled and red. There'd been a touch of hurt in his voice—as if contentment had been a slur on his master's memory. I think Dr. Newby had been about to take him up—when all conversation stopped. Lady Dexter was abruptly of the company. She wore black, which rustled like leaves—and set off the whiteness of her face strikingly.

"If you were talking of my husband, gentlemen—I beg of you, don't stop on my account. For I'd rather have him talked about now, on this evil day . . . even to air his soul, if you will . . . than to have him spoke of tomorrow, or next week . . . or year . . . or ever after again. Joseph, Dr. Newby, Mr. Treet . . . ah! My brother-in-law and Mr. Craddock! All of you—talk him out of your hearts and minds and lives! And then have done—"

"Sister," said the new Lady Dexter, warningly. "Would this not be better without—er—strangers?" She looked very coolly at Mr. Treet and me.

"Madam," replied Lady Dexter, with an odd sadness in her eyes—though her voice was sharp as ever, "even my husband was courteous to strangers. And to let the young man understand how and why his short life was made so free with—even nearly ended—is the least courtesy we can offer. For I'd not have him carry away an ill image of all of us!"

· 18 ·

"His heart was diseased—for longer than we guessed," said Dr. Newby—who was acquainted with such things . . . and was confined to them.

"He was mad—and fit for Bedlam," the Captain had declared—for he'd been near madness himself . . . maybe in Newgate, and then at his wits' end in the copse.

"He was a man who tried to purchase a freehold by mortgaging his soul," said the lawyer. "It was the entail that did for him." For, to Mr. Craddock, a man's soul was no more than a plain leasehold, poked into a foggy office . . . to be canceled on completion . . . and with no clause for redecoration.

"He was one of the dark Dexters," said Joseph, simply. "Every now and then, there is such a one. I thought at first it was Mr. Richard . . . for the smell of corrosion was strong in the house. But it was my master who suffered from that infection. Great gentlemen, when they suffer, suffer greatly—and die in proportion to their natures."

For to Joseph, death had leveled no one but the living. . . .

His madness, darkness, disease, or enmity with death—what you will—had taken the form of hatred and contempt for his brother, who, he dreaded, would one day inherit. Thus the deaths of his first three sons in pitiful infancy seemed unnaturally bitter. (Lady Dexter's face was hard and cold with memories.) Which bitterness nourished his disease with new poison. And when his brother married—none too nobly, either—and set about producing healthy male child after male child, his spiritual torment grew intense. ("He'd no right!" muttered the brand-new Lady Dexter. "For my family— though it winds and twines a bit—goes back like his, to Adam and Eve! To insult me was to insult himself! Ain't that so, Sir Richard?")

When his brother's first child was christened John he took it, not as a gesture of peace, goodwill, and affection, but as a grim omen (maybe even deliberate) that when he, Sir John, should die, his place would be took and Death would consume him utterly. But none of this inward gnawing ever showed, for, as Joseph said, "He was a Dexter—and even in the face of Hell, could smile."

Then came a sunny time in his life . . . for he had a son who survived: George. Frail, sickly, yet sleeping and waking, day after day . . . week after week. The entail was defeated—and Sir John's hatred slept. Though he never courted his brother's friendship, now he did not reject it. For a brief while the house was cheerful— and the younger Dexter family visited. . . . (Which circumstance was turned afterward to a sinister advantage.)

Six months . . . nine months . . . to the very edge of

a year, George Dexter breathed, cried, and sometimes smiled. And then—he died.

"He must have discovered it about six o'clock," said Dr. Newby. "For I remember now, he left the party and was away some minutes before returning, curiously white. I remember clearly thinking how suddenly ill he looked . . . and considered begging him to retire. Then, d'you recall, he said he'd to ride over to Poynings for an hour?

"And he was able to smile! Extraordinary! With that great burden on his brain . . . crushing out every other thought! Consider that burden—and marvel at the mind that sustained it!

"He'd gone to his son's room—on an impulse of affection or pride. Crept in, one supposes—for the nurse never woke. Sees her sleeping. Likewise, his son. For death, in infants, is very deceiving. . . . He stares into the cot . . . smiling, one supposes. Then—another sudden impulse of paternal pride. He desires to show off his heir. He'll carry him down below. Excellent notion! His health will be drunk—for it's his birthday! He reaches down. He touches the child. He recoils. The child is cold. The child is dead!

"Gentlemen—consider his horror, his dismay, the sudden rush of overwhelming bitterness that Fate, in a shape so mean and despicable, should topple him into the abyss! But he did not go mad . . . not in the true and medical sense."

"He was never mad!" exclaimed Joseph.

"He was Bedlam-mad," muttered his brother, shivering. "No one but a madman would have done what he did! Went downstairs. Continued in company as though naught had happened. Then went back to the death room. Took out the child. Hid it, maybe, under his coat. What a secret! Then bore it out of the house and buried it madly in the copse . . . as if to conceal that the child was dead—not only from the world, but from himself! If that's not madness, what other name d'you give it? Horrible, horrible scene!"

So the little George Dexter vanished from his cot, vanished from his room . . . and all the agony of searching went on—led by Sir John himself—till he went to London on the day following and saw Mr. Craddock.

"He never confessed the death," said the lawyer. "Else I'd not have been party to it. He was my Principal, and it was my duty to believe in him when he spoke of his child's abduction. Naturally, I was sanguine of the infant's speedy return—for a price—and did not at first credit absolutely that the younger brother was involved. But my Principal was insistent, and it was my duty to give him, not his opponent, the benefit of doubt.

"Therefore, the following scheme was proposed between us against the chance of his son's not being recovered, for my Principal was fiercely determined that a villain should not profit by his villainy. Which is good law, besides having been my Principal's desire. I was to find a child of similar age and coloring, and purchase that infant at the rate of sixty pound a year— payable on the third day of June and November—till such time as the true son was recovered. In which event I was to conclude the above-mentioned agreement with a payment of five hundred pound. But if— for one reason or another—the true son was *not* recovered, my instructions were to say, "My Principal bids me come no more. By which it was understood that the child was to be delivered to Sir John, hope having been abandoned for the other.

"I do not say this scheme was hit on at once. Indeed, it was the outcome of much debate and consultation . . . for that is what an attorney is for—to guide, advise, and help . . . but always, in the end, to obey his Principal."

"So you lied about everything, sir!" I said bitterly to my father, Mr. Treet. "Even about the Stranger in the storm with the child."

"But there was a storm, my dear. And—and as for the little one—well, in a manner of speaking, it was so—"

"That's just what it wasn't, sir! 'In a manner of speaking,' it was absolutely not so!"

"He brought a bundle . . . which looked, at first, as though it hid a child—but 'twas only linen and toys. . . . George, my dear . . . don't be mistook in me. For I loved you dearly and—"

"And sold me, sir? My name was George, not Joseph!"

Mr. Treet looked momentarily angry—then shook his head. "Indeed, I loved you, and believed that, if ever you was called in, you'd be better provided for than ever I could manage. Besides," he went on, brightening into his usual self, "I considered it would all come to nothing—and we'd be better off by whatever the gentleman brought. I believed it to be for the best, my dear, and you must judge me accordingly."

Plainly thinking he'd come out of it well, he looked round for approval. But from me, he got none. There was something else. . . .

"The scar, Mr. Treet, sir. How come I was scarred?"

He looked awkward. A rare thing for Mr. Treet. "I swear to you, my eldest son, I did not wound your darling head. *That*, I could never have done."

"Then who . . . ?"

"The legal gentleman, dear child! With a penknife."

"And—and you stood by while it was done?"

"No, sir!" said Mr. Treet, with some dignity. "I left the room and stopped up my ears. Even for thirty pound twice a year I could not have stood by for *that*!"

"And my mother . . . ?"

"Not present. In Shoreham at the time."

"Then thank God I had *one* honorable parent!"

Vastly outraged by Mr. Treet's confession, I shook his hand off my shoulder . . . and considered myself to've been the most misused one-year-old since the days of King Herod!

So the bargain had been struck, and thereafter, for thirteen years, Mr. Treet was paid my rent every June and November. The gloom this caused him, he said, he pushed—between rent days—to the back of his mind, which place must have been the largest of its kind anywhere.

And for thirteen years, Sir John Dexter spread the tale of his brother's monstrous guilt. (Here, the Captain frowned at the memory of much scorn, contempt, and consequent privation . . . together with a general sinking of self-esteem till he was forced to seek company where esteem was of no account. He glanced to his lady—who'd shared much with him—and gently shook his head, as if to say, "But now, my dear, we'll lift our heads again. . . .")

"Nonetheless," said Dr. Newby, "I believe, had it not been for his fatal condition, he would have gone no further than that. For it was only when I told him— warned him—that he'd little to expect . . . that something like madness—'like,' I say, for it was never true madness in the medical sense!—something like true madness supervened."

He conceived the notion of the duel, doubtless in the hope of being killed—men, when a period is put to their lives, often grow impatient. . . . And, in the event of his death—which he must have both hoped for and dreaded—he'd instructed Mr. Craddock that his brother should be arraigned for his murder . . . and the Treet boy fetched to the house. Thus the ruin of his brother and that maligned man's family was to be utter and complete.

"He was, after all, my Principal," explained Mr. Craddock.

"He must have been the Devil!" cried the new Lady Dexter.

"No, madam—his heart was diseased . . . believe me . . . that was the cause."

But though he was not killed (he'd fallen into the path of the bullet, but had misjudged), he believed himself to've been mortally wounded, so Mr. Craddock was instructed nonetheless. He went to Sandwich, to the Eloquent Gentlewoman, and said:

"My Principal bids me come no more."

"It was a blow to my heart," murmured Mr. Treet. "For I never believed it would happen. But I thought of you, George . . . and the love, riches, and benefits that might be yours. For I knew even less of the truth than Mr. Craddock, and always suspected him to've been the Principal himself . . . maybe making some sort of amends. . . ."

So Sir John lay waiting, day after day, keeping open house so's none might be turned away . . . waiting for the rented child to be brought, the purchase to be completed, and the entail made secure.

"I fulfilled my obligation," said Mr. Craddock.

"And so did I," murmured Mr. Treet, and Lady Dexter looked from one to the other of them with the profoundest irony her pale, handsome face could contrive.

"Then who failed?" she asked coldly. "The deceived mother, or the deceived child?"

"Begging your ladyship's pardon—and yours, Mr. George, sir," said Joseph, quietly, "but it was my good master who failed."

And then that strange, conspiratorial, but profoundly faithful servant told of what he believed to've been his master's last tragedy—the revenge of truth.

For Lady Dexter—though at first she might have doubted—even suspected Mr. Treet of chicanery—came to believe in (though always protecting herself with irony against disappointment), and even to love her son, for her life hitherto had been much deprived of that commodity, and the chance of it now was not to be missed. . . .

"And you, Mr. George, sir—you believed. I saw you striving, with all your heart's might, to be worthy of the fine gentleman you took to be your father. And I sensed it did not please him."

All my accomplishments, Joseph said, all my skills, brightness, strength, and affection—here, I saw Mr. Treet smile proudly—which the world saw as excellence in a new Dexter, Sir John saw only as the properties of a mountebank's child. (Here, Mr. Treet frowned, and withdrew somewhat.) For, though he was willing to deceive the world, he could not—when faced with his scheme—deceive himself. Nor could he deceive the dead. . . .

Many times had Joseph come upon him shrunk in loneliness in the library . . . not reading, but staring up at the painted Dexters—who must have known the secret of his heart. How he must have dreaded them! How they must have haunted him . . . stalking his dreams . . . glaring in through windows . . . stepping stiffly out of shadows . . . pointing, mouthing, "We are not deceived. You are betraying your birthright. You are betraying us."

Joseph fell silent, and I glanced up at the flat, smiling Dexters . . . and shivered.

So he'd determined on killing me—being too far gone in deception to withdraw. And yet—I still believe him to've had some second thoughts . . . even after the quarrel I'd had with his nephew (which must have racked him). For, though he gave me the murderously cracked pistol, he gave me also the thirty pound extra, plainly in the hope I'd use it to go off with the Treets. For the man he'd paid to waylay me was only to do so if I should return.

My God! He must have been tormented when he heard the shot . . . and then hideously shaken when I came back! For he knew then he'd have to accomplish the murder with his own hand. And still, even when set on the meanest and blackest act a man's capable of, he kept to his mad pride! I'll never forget the look on his face before the pistol burst it . . . the beginnings of contempt, I mean. For he must have imagined I was pleading for my own life—not trying to save his. I'm sorry about that, for I always tried very hard to have him think well of me, and at no time—even when I knew the truth—was I careless of that opinion. If Mrs. Montague ever talks with him (which I doubt, for she feared him alive, and still fears him dead), I hope she sets him right on that score. . . .

He is buried in Fulking churchyard, and his portrait—

painted when young—has been moved to a darker wall, where it remains, even in high summer, much shadowed. But sometimes, when the light catches it, it seems to have the same strained, uneasy smile as the others . . . as if there was an obscure jest that the Dexters never understood, but always thought it gentlemanly to smile at.

Mr. Treet stood up.

"Come, George, my son. Your brothers and sisters will wonder what's become of us."

I looked at him, standing beside me like a pillar of all the virtues, supporting absolutely nothing. I felt very bitter toward Mr. Treet.

"Yes, indeed, sir. For they might begin to think you'd sold *them* to the landlord of the Shepherd and Dog. I hope, sir, we are still seven? Or has Hotspur, maybe, been sold to the Prince of Wales? For I'll have you all know we only go to good homes!"

"George! I'm your father—"

"Which makes it ten times worse! I'll not forgive you, sir! Not ever!"

"George—"

"I don't know how you manage to be a great man, sir! For you are—and don't deserve to be!"

"Maybe a—a blind spot, dear boy? We all have one . . . a blind spot—"

"A blind *spot*, sir? Good God! 'Tis a whole rash!"

"George—"

"And now you expect me to return to you—"

"George—"

Suddenly, my friend, the Captain, spoke:

"If it could be arranged, I'd be proud to call you 'son,' George—"

"Papa!" Bertram Dexter, scarlet with rage: "He's a vagabond—"

"Be silent! I'd change fifty of you for him! And let me warn you, sir—one more headache or bellyache and Dr. Newby here will purge you with pills like grape-shot! For George was my friend when I was a fugitive! While you, sir—just the thought of you—was a chain round my heart! Well, sir"—to Mr. Treet—"will you consent?"

"Mr. Treet—brother." Lady Dexter, her face pale, her smile as ironical as ever: "If this boy is . . . a marketable commodity, I—I believe I have the first claim. I can give him much, Mr. Treet. Think carefully, sir. Think kindly, George."

I felt very moved, for I'd not thought Lady Dexter to've been so fond. . . . Mr. Treet shuffled his feet. Looked mightily awkward. Furtive, almost—as if wishing the offers had been made in private.

"Another thousand pound," said Lady Dexter, softly.

"Two thousand," bid my friend, the Captain—who'd not yet paid back what he owed!

Mr. Treet looked at me. He shrugged his broad shoulders. His eyes were quite moist. He smiled help-lessly. (To be angry with Mr. Treet was not possible.)

"We Treets," he said, "are like eagles. We wheel and turn and tumble and sing in the upper air. Even our fledglings. Kind friends—what could you do for an eagle—save give him a golden cage? Have you ever seen the spirits grow in 'Lucifer's Smoke'? George has. Have you ever seen the angels in 'Devil's Fire'? George has. Do you know the properties of Berlin Syrup, or Crystals of Lemon? George does. Would you have me rob him again of these, and all the triumphs to come? No, good people. George Treet is my son—and not for sale!"

When he'd finished my eyes were fairly afloat with tears! Not on account of my father's speech (and here, don't imagine I belittle him, for he was a great orator, capable of moving more than his son), but on a deeper account than that! I was truly weeping for joy! (And I assure you, it happens!) For it seemed that only then did I understand that my golden past was to be my golden future as well! That once more I had three brothers and three sisters . . . and that the Treet family was again Mr. Treet and a full seven geniuses! To say nothing of Otway, our remarkable horse!

But to return to Mr. Treet and his great speech. I looked at him in all his sheepish glory . . . and could not directly speak. I saw him look uncertain—even faintly bewildered—and still the words would not come. Then Lady Dexter put her arm on my shoulder and said, very unequally:

"Now you've discovered Mr. Treet is not the blackest of villains, dear George—don't be mortified that he's not been the brightest of saints, either! There's something in between you know! So forgive him—for I'm sure he's a great man in spite of all!"

I must have smiled and nodded . . . for Mr. Treet smiled, too, and said, "George . . . George . . ." five or six times over, as if it was a name that moved him to particular joy.

And still I could not speak—not even to make my genteel farewells! To be honest, I'd really begun to fear I'd lost my powers of eloquence!

And I could not stop smiling, try as I might. Desperately I sought to fix my mind on all manner of grim and melancholy thoughts—to look serious as the general situation demanded—but a strong detachment of cheerfulness enfiladed every effort! For a moment I nearly succeeded—till I glanced through the window and saw, upon the wide, smooth green, six of the most talented personages in the land approaching in a dancing line! And smiling broke in again . . . so I spread out my hands, and bowed.

"Before you go, George," called Sir Richard Dexter, "always remember that I'd have been proud to call you my son!"

"Before you, go, Mr. George, sir," added Joseph, "always remember that I'm sorry that you're not!"

"And remember us!" cried Mr. Rumbold, who'd not long arrived. "I promise you Mrs. Rumbold and the children won't be surprised! For we all thought you was more of a prince than a Dexter!"

Lady Dexter did not, at that time, make her own farewell, for she was to visit us all in the Shepherd and Dog that afternoon (which honor nearly split the landlord's breeches with bowing and scraping).

And even then she made no firm farewell, but spoke of a "mysterious plan" she had in mind, the very mysteriousness of which, coming from a lady of so ancient a family, interested Edward enormously. Hotspur, of course, could not be kept quiet but kept plaguing her with his jumpings up and down and shouts of:

"A thecret! A thecret! Tell uth your thecret!"

But she only laughed and shook her finger at him and told him he'd have to be patient else she'd put him to bed herself!

I think Jane impressed her most of all—on account of Jane's great good sense and gentleness of manner, while on the other hand, Rose Treet was most impressed by her ladyship, who, she judged, had at least ten thousand a year in her own right! Then Lady Dexter beckoned Mr. Treet aside and she and he remained in conversation for a long while.

It wasn't long before we discovered what Lady Dexter's secret plan was—for she put it into execution almost at once. (But not before Mr. Treet had half given it away, for he's a great horror of secrets now!) She was to remove to a fashionable house in London, for the chief purpose of patronizing Mr. Treet and the rest of us, as she considers us a most valuable and worthy investment for her fortune and interest!

She was in London within the week—almost to the day when we arrived ourselves. And, since that time, has always been as firm, strong, and sometimes ironical a friend as could be found anywhere in the world. Her interest and concern never changes, and, when we're away, she always demands news and insists that I write often and seal my letters with the ring she once gave me.

From time to time she advances Mr. Treet capital— never a great sum, but always sufficient. And each time she says, with her cool smile:

"Be provident, sir. Be more shrewd. Greatness is not enough. I *insist*, sir, you be more moderate—particularly with Crystals of Lemon! Else next time I'll come with you!"

My own consequence in the family has, of course, improved as a result of my two months' high nobility. Even Edward now defers to me on questions of law and lineage, and Rose on questions of wealth. Henry has a great respect for me upon weapons, and Jane upon manners, deportment, and air. While to Hotspur I am now "George, the gentleman geniuth."

*   *   *

Back in Fulking, the house, I understand, is now somewhat cheerfuller with its new possessors . . . though it will always be dark, and the mists will always inhabit the copse. But at least that uneasy place's chief inhabitant has now been moved. For the dead little gentleman sleeps in the churchyard close by his father—and talks to Mrs. Montague no more.